Patrick Leigh Fermor

Patrick Leigh Fermor was born in 1915 of English and Irish descent. He was only eighteen when he set off to walk from the Hook of Holland to Constantinople, a now famous journey described many years later in *A Time of Gifts* and *Between the Woods and the Water*. The third volume in the trilogy is still awaited. He enlisted in the Irish Guards in 1939 and fought in Greece and Crete, where, disguised as a shepherd, he lived for over two years in the mountains organizing the resistance. In 1944 he led the party that captured the German Commander General Kreipe, an event immortalised in the film *Ill Met by Moonlight*, starring Dirk Bogarde. He was awarded the OBE in 1943 and the DSO in 1944. Patrick Leigh Fermor's books have won many awards including the W H Smith Literary Award, the Thomas Cook Travel Award and the Duff Cooper Memorial Prize. He now lives partly in Greece in the house he designed with his wife Joan in an olive grove in the Mani, and partly in Worcestershire.

By the same author

THE TRAVELLER'S TREE
A TIME TO KEEP SILENCE
MANI
ROUMELI
A TIME OF GIFTS
BETWEEN THE WOODS AND THE WATER
WORDS OF MERCURY

Patrick Leigh Fermor

The Violins of Saint-Jacques

A TALE OF THE ANTILLES

John Murray

First published in Great Britain in 1953
by André Deutsch Ltd
and John Murray (Publishers)
A division of Hodder Headline

Paperback edition 2004

5

A CIP catalogue record for this title is available from the British Library

ISBN 978-0-7195-5529-9

Printed and bound in Great Britain by Clays Ltd, St Ives plc.

John Murray (Publishers)
338 Euston Road
London
NW1 3BH

TO

DIANA COOPER

Pte à Pitre

Pte des

Guadeloupe

Châteaux

Petit Cul de Sac Martin

Souffriere Ste Marie

16°

Trois Rivières

Marie

Grande Anse   Pte de Folléanse

Galante

Caribbean Sea

Grande Bourg

MN

Islands of the Saints

N

Cape Melville   Pte Baptiste

Portsmouth   Crumpton

Prince Rupert Bay   Pt

Dominica   Pagou

61°

Petite Terre

Ilot des Faives

Atlantic

Cap
d'Ivry

Plessis

Salpetrière

Ocean

Etang du Cacique

Anse Caraibe

Morne d'Esnambuq

Saint - Jacques des Alisés

Pte d'Estaing

Ilot Vache

Infelix domus . . . sonitu tremibunda profundi.
Valerius Flaccus

Little distinguishes the history of the small island from that of the other French Windward and Leeward Isles except that less is known about it. Saint-Jacques was originally inhabited by the Arawak Indians, later by the fierce Caribs who mounted the island chain in dugout canoes, defeated and devoured the Arawak men and then married their widows in their usual brisk way. Columbus discovered it on his second voyage and annexed it to the Spanish crown. The Carib name of Twahleiba – the Snake – derived from the terrible trigonocephalus that infested it in swarms – was changed, and the island was christened in honour of the great Spanish saint of Compostella on the vigil of whose feast the island was captured. *Santiago de los Vientos Alicios*, they pricked it down on those early charts; Saint James of the Trade Winds. (Later on it was facetiously known, in the cant of the English filibusters who haunted the inlets of the northern coast, as Jack of All Trades and occasionally, in chanties that are seldom heard nowadays, as Tradey Jack.)

The name appears on few of the old Spanish charts preserved in the archives at Seville, and on French and English maps of the time even less. Cartographer and historian unconsciously conspired to ignore it. Father Labat never called there and the only monkish chronicler to mention it is an obscure Franciscan missionary from Treviso, Father Jerome Zancarol. The Father enlarges in queer jargon on the island's richness in sugar-cane, rum, molasses and indigo but says little that is complimentary to the inhabitants. *Insula Sancti Jacobi*, he writes, *tantis opibus, tanta copia, tantaque pulchritudine ornata, sicut angulus coeli ipsius videtur, sed, ob mores improbos pravosque incolarum, ob jactanciam, luxuriam et gastrimargiam et Gallorum et nigrorum, insula Sancti Jacobi pessimam insularum aliarum omnium justius, immo, verum angulum Gehennae putanda est*;[1] and no more.

The small island was neglected by Spain, settled by a certain chevalier Hippolyte-Hercule du Plessis, an illegitimate kinsman of Richelieu, and annexed to France. Plessis, after whom the capital was named, exterminated the stiff-necked Caribs, imported the first slaves from Africa and summoned and enfeoffed a swarm of penniless cadets of noble French families from Normandy, Brittany, Gascony and the Vendée to colonise the island; and, in its small way, Saint-Jacques soon rivalled Sainte-Domingue and Martinique in prosperity. Rumbold and his West Indian Light Fencibles captured it in the Seven Years' War, and, until the Revolution, the Union Jack

1. *De Rebus Insularum Indiarum Occidentis quae Charaeibae vel Karaibi Dicuntur*. Rev P. Heiron. Zancarolus, O.S.F., 7 Vols. Venice, 1723.

flew from a beautiful little Palladian government house, built by Sir Probyn Scudamore and later enlarged by Governor Braithwaite, in the capital which was now re-baptised Jamestown. The English were thrown out at the time of the Convention. During the Terror the guillotine was set up in the Place Hercule, but, when the bright blade descended and the first royalist head fell into the basket, a cry of horror burst from the silent throng of negroes. Breaking through the cordon of guards, they tore the instrument to bits, and the guillotine was never re-erected in Saint-Jacques.[1] A tumultuous period ensued. Order was restored during the Consulate and Saint-Jacques des Alisés thereafter followed the same quiet course as the other French Antilles.

The islet seems to have been less affected than its larger neighbours by the decline of the sugar plantations after the Emancipation Act of '48 – perhaps because of its remoteness, perhaps because the island squirearchy lived on better terms with the negroes. At all events, by the turn of the century, Zancarol's accusations of wickedness would have seemed exaggerated. Little was known about Saint-Jacques in the rest of the archipelago, in fact the very name – except for the fabulous beauty of its mountains and forests, the elegance of the old buildings, the charm of the inhabitants and the brio with which they availed themselves of the slightest pretext for enjoyment and celebration – seems to have slipped the attention of travellers. It also appears that Saint-Jacques was distinguished by more than a tincture of

1. The same phenomenon occurred in Haiti.

polite learning. The works of Aimable Bruno, the mulatto poet of the island, are unfortunately lost to us. Lost too are the many portraits of Jacobean notables by Hubert Clamart (a pupil of Liotard), which adorned the private houses and the public buildings of Plessis. It is a little mysterious, all this being so, that Lafcadio Hearn should never have visited Saint-Jacques during his Caribbean sojourn. How brilliantly he would have described those vanished Jacobean festivities! As it is, alas, the data are few. About the absence of the name of Saint-Jacques from the atlas page – a few leagues windward from the channel that flows between Guadeloupe and Dominica and well to the south-east of Marie Galante, where it hung like a bead on the sixty-first meridian – there is, tragically, no mystery at all. But so formidable are the obstacles in the path of research and so complete the decay of the archives in the European Capitals that writers on the Caribbean have all been forced, through ignorance of its history and, all too often, of its former existence, to omit it.

*　　*　　*

It was in another island, thousands of miles from the Antilles, that I met the person who was to bring to life this vanished world, and especially that baleful and culminating night that singles it out from oblivion.

I first came upon Berthe de Rennes under an umbrella pine on a headland in Mitylene two years ago. She was sitting on a rock with a cigarette in one hand and in the other a brush with which she painted the blue-veined shadows of the Asia Minor coast (which lay just over the water) on a block of cartridge paper propped on an easel. She wore a blue cotton dress and sandals, and her grey hair was uncompromisingly arranged. Her intelligent, hawkish and most distinguished face was shaded by one of those broad wicker-hats the Ægean peasants wear in summer. I assumed she was somewhere in her fifties and was surprised to learn, later on, that she was well over seventy. Seeing me hunting in vain for a match, she threw me her lighter to catch – a rough peasant one with a dangling foot and a half of orange wick – almost without looking away from her picture. We were soon in conversation. She talked a lively, descriptive, rather racy French, and her English was of a fluent Edwardian kind scattered with expressions obsolete long enough to be full of charm. Her tales of life in Mitylene, of brushes with the nomarch and the bishop, and, later on, her reminiscences of Fiji and Rara Tonga, Corsica and the Balearics and finally, to my redoubled interest, of the Caribbean from which I had just come back, were interjected every now and then by a deep and oddly attractive laugh with a slight rasp in it, and it soon became clear that she was an excellent mimic. She had a very beautiful voice.

As she talked she went on painting with an un-erring competence, screwing her eyes up in aquiline glances at the fading Lydian hills. There was nothing vague or old-maidish about the picture. Bold, fluid pen-strokes outlined the trees and the mountains, the forest of caïque masts below and the distant villages. They were depicted with a swift and out-of-date precision and then filled in with sweeping washes of water-colour rather in the manner of Edward Lear. When it became too dark to paint, an antelope-eyed girl approached on bare feet over the pine needles and began to collect her painting things. 'What a goose that girl is!' Mademoiselle de Rennes sighed. 'I tell her every day not to come, but she turns up just the same. She seems to think I'm a hundred.' Our paths lay in opposite directions but before we separated she asked me to come to luncheon at her little house next day and 'take pot luck'. I watched them disappear through the olive groves. Mademoiselle de Rennes was taller standing than I had suspected. Phrosoula padded beside her holding the Asia Minor landscape as though it were a processional ikon.

Drinking a last ouzo before a lonely dinner on the waterfront, I asked the waiter about the French lady who lived outside the town. He sat down at once. 'Kyria Mpertha? She has travelled the whole world over and seen everything. It must be about twenty years ago that she settled here to teach the young ladies of the island French and how to draw and play the piano.' His fingers rattled along an imaginary keyboard. 'She was very poor then, but she still does it a bit, out of pleasure, as it were. And they say she is a wonderful teacher. And intelligent and energetic! Like gunpowder! Everybody likes her, from the governor to the bootblack. And she won't stand any nonsense. We had a bad town clerk here once who quarrelled with her, the fool. You should have seen how quickly she got rid of him! *Po, po, po!* He vanished faster than the dew. She has got more to her than most of the people you see about the place in trousers.'

★　　★　　★

Mademoiselle de Rennes lived in a white, thick-walled island house surrounded by flowers in ribbed white amphoræ and by pots of marjoram and basil. The headland on which it rested overlooked a steep bay and a wide stretch of the Ægean bounded on the east by the watersheds of Anatolia and to the south by the floating ghosts of Samos and Chios. Mademoiselle de Rennes, with heavy horn-rimmed glasses across the high bridge of her nose, was reading in a deck-chair under a vine trellis. Phrosoula, the girl of the evening before, soon appeared carrying a table that was already laid, and 'pot luck' turned out to be the best meal I had eaten for months. The wine, too, from the surrounding vineyards which Mademoiselle de Rennes had tended for years, was excellent. The conversation ranged all over the world once more and ended with a long and diverting account of some pre-fascist elections in Cagliari. She asked me for news of the French West Indies, but she herself was less expansive about them than the many other islands in which she had lived. Even under the shade of the trellis, the afternoon was soon so hot and sleepy that I gratefully accepted my hostess's offer of a room for a siesta.

After the sunlight the inside of the house seemed pitch dark and it took a minute for my eyes to acclimatise themselves. My room was empty except for a bed and a large, faded painting, obviously by my hostess. It was the picture of a volcanic island painted from a ship or a raft a few furlongs out to sea. Beyond the swarming sloops and schooners and a white paddle steamer, a long quay stretched, where turbaned negresses presided over stalls of tropical fruit under brilliant awnings. Beyond this lay a main street where carriages of every kind plied up and down. Women with parasols and men in boaters and top hats were poised in cushioned aloofness over thin-spoked wheels. Below them bustled a swarm of negroes with pyramids of fruit or bright green sheaves of sugar-cane on their heads. All were dominated by a scattered population, hoisted high on their rococo pedestals, of grey and gravely gesticulating statues. Further back still, beyond a row of elaborate gasoliers, arcaded streets receded in vistas that climbed the hillside through successive strata of eighteenth-century terraces. Their balustrades were lined with urns and statuettes, and awnings shaded many of the windows. The bells of half a dozen church towers were suspended in wrought-iron hampers above roofs of semicircular rose-coloured tiles, and at the summit of the little metropolis, corresponding to a bastion and a lighthouse at the end of the mole, the round tower of a fort aimed cannon from its battlements like the truncated radii of a compass. A tricolour fluttered from the flag-pole; slender palm stems raised pretty pale green mops; a froth of creeper and hibiscus overflowed the walls. Above the town, a tropical forest rose in a cone, hiding to its crater the steep and concave flanks of a volcano from whose blunt apex curled a languid blue-grey banner of smoke.

'It's the last thing I painted in the Antilles,' said Mademoiselle Berthe as she closed the shutters. 'It's not too bad.'

When she had left I looked at it more closely. In one corner the signature was neatly inscribed in ink: *B. de Rennes*, 1902, and in the other, to my suddenly heightening excitement: *Fort de Plessis, Le Mouillage et la Salpetrière, Saint-Jacques des Alisés.* Outside, the scraping of the cicadas rose and fell and a single arrow of sunlight, penetrating the cool shuttered gloom, sent a bright shaft across the towers and statues of Plessis. By the time that I fell asleep in a mood of vague conjecture about the mysterious little town, the trajectory of its aim had slanted upwards to the Salpetrière's smoking cone.

* * *

During the next two weeks, not a day passed without my calling at least once on Mademoiselle Berthe. I would walk along the shore and bathe in the late afternoon and climb to her terrace at ouzo time. Often I stayed to dinner and we would talk till late. She was delightful company and the distant Caribbean island I had never seen, but which she described so lucidly, remains far clearer in retrospect than the beautiful Ægean

one in which we were sitting. Berthe seemed to enjoy
these long sessions and the chance of talking to someone
who had a slight knowledge of the distant waters where
much of her youth had been spent. She had a gift for
conversational autobiography and I soon had a clear
outline of her life.

She belonged to an old and impoverished *chouan*
family of the lower Vendée. An only child, she was
brought up in a semi-castellated manor house in that flat
green region. Her father, an ex-colonel in the colonial
cavalry, died before she had grown up and left her in the
care of an equally impoverished aunt, a lay-canoness
living in Paris. Unwilling to be a burden on her she
accepted the offer of a distant relation to act as governess
to his children in the faraway Caribbean island of Saint-
Jacques. She had never met these *cousins à la mode de
Bretagne*, but she made ready without hesitation, caught
the packet from le Havre to Guadeloupe, where she
took the fortnightly paddle steamer – the same that
appeared in the picture – to Plessis: no mean feat for a
girl of eighteen in the 1890's. The entire Serindan family
were waiting for her on the quay: a handsome middle-
aged couple, a tall boy in his early teens, three girls in
huge hats ranging downwards at varying intervals and
a little boy. A voluminous negress held him by the hand
and a mongoose's head peered out of the collar of his
sailor suit. They all kissed her and called her 'Cousine
Berthe' and the little boy gave her his mongoose to
hold. Negro servants hoisted her meagre luggage on to
their heads and trotted away, and the party piled into

an immense landau. A smart negro coachman cracked his whip and away they bowled up the steep main street.

I could never tire of hearing her stories about the life of the island. She stayed in Saint-Jacques six years and, had the fortunes of the island turned out more propitiously, she might have been there still. She was entirely happy. Her descriptions were illustrated by a number of commonplace-books and albums of sketches and paintings which she had filled, apparently, for the amusement of her old aunt in Paris, despatching each one on its completion, and receiving them all back years later on her aunt's death. There were about a dozen, and, at my entreaty, she had fished them out of a trunk and lent them to me. How much more alive and revealing they were than the single photograph-album which had also survived! There was one photograph, however, to which I often turned back: one of Berthe herself, a slim girl in a riding habit buttoned up to the neck in the fashion of Winterhalter's heroines of a few decades earlier. Her gloved hands were folded over an elegant riding switch. A preposterous curly-brimmed billycock, nesting behind on a heavy golden coil of plaits, was tilted forward over slightly frowning brows and wide eyes set in a grave and lovely face. The photograph had faded to the pallor of khaki drill and insects had freckled it with little holes; yet the fine bone-structure was unmistakably that of the slightly sardonic but still rather beautiful features opposite, which the summer sun of Greece had burnt to an almost Red Indian hue and made her large grey eyes seem still clearer and more luminous.

The sketch-books covered the entire life of the island. All the fine buildings of the capital were there, the statues of Plessis and Rumbold and Scudamore and Braithwaite and Schœlcher[1]; views of savannah and volcanic ravine and stifling forest; punctilious flower-paintings of hibiscus and balisier, of looping lianas, tree-ferns and dark branches where the Night Flowering Cereus grew. Even the monuments and inscriptions of churches were copied down. There was an abundance of negroes and negresses in their brilliant village costumes and flamboyantly disguised for carnival. There were indentured Hindu labourers in saris and many silver bracelets; scenes from the markets and the plantations among lakes of plumed sugar-cane; the estates and the curiously named *gentilhommières* of the island's creole oligarchy, and their inhabitants. As I listened and slowly turned the pages, the life of this happy, patrician, slightly provincial minority, into the heart of which Mademoiselle Berthe had suddenly been propelled, took shape. How leisurely and remote it all sounded! The cohorts of negro servants, the balls and the races, the long rides in cavalcades twenty or thirty strong; the picnics by the ever-smouldering cone of the Salpetrière, the love-affairs and quarrels and duels and reconciliations and marriages; the glimmering indoor life of the rainy season; the lazy afternoons in hammocks

1. The French Wilberforce.

slung between mango trees and the hot nights under milky pavilions of muslin.

The Serindans were drawn so often and Berthe described them in such lucid detail that I soon felt I had known them all for a long time. The family, and indeed the whole of Saint-Jacques, was benevolently dominated by her distant cousin, Count Raoul-Agénor-Marie-Gaëtan de Serindan de la Charce-Fontenay (Berthe smiled as she repeated the prodigious name), the owner of Beauséjour, which was the richest and largest of the Jacobean estates. The Count de Serindan was a descendant of Plessis in the female line, and, though a scorner of Napoleon (and, for that matter, of the Orléans family, which, he often declared, were a band of upstarts and a disgrace to the House of

France), he would frequently mention his kinship with Josephine de Tacher of nearby Martinique, the victim of that lamentable Corsican *mésalliance*; and old prints of the ruins of La Pagerie hung on the walls. The news of the death of the Comte de Chambord had struck the Count's ears like a knell and a black crape ribbon still adorned a lilied shield in his study.

The Serindans were related to all the French families of the archipelago and their affiliations spread as far afield as the Guianas and Louisiana and Quebec; even to Nova Scotia – or rather, as he still insisted on calling it, to Acadie. Their position in Saint-Jacques was Olympian. The church at Beauséjour, which had been unroofed by a score of hurricanes and a score of times roofed over again, was walled and paved with memorial slabs, each topped by a stone helmet with its frozen foliage of mantelling and the emblems of dead Serindans. The orgulous record of their gestures – the carnage they had wrought among the Caribs and the English, their Christian virtues, the multitude of their progeny, their valour in attack and their impavid patience in adversity, the suavity of their manners, the splendour of their munificence and their pious ends – was incised with a swirling seventeenth-century duplication of long S's and a cumulative nexus of dog-Latin superlatives that hissed from the shattered slabs like a basketful of snakes.

In company with the other creole landowners the Count was not only exaggeratedly vain of his family's long history in the island and its total freedom from any coloured admixture – though not all of them, Berthe darkly interjected, could be equally sure on this head – but of its freedom from unarmigerous alliances. Again like his Jacobean compeers, he had frequent outbursts against the Third Republic – a band, he would affirm, flinging both hands into the air, of robbers, atheists, freemasons, Jacobins, traitors, and, at the beginning of the *Affaire*, filthy Dreyfusards. He had been known to box one of his children's ears for whistling the Marseillaise, a tune which sounded as balefully to him as *Ça ira* or the *Carmagnole*. The revolution alone, he would thunder, was to blame not only for the atheism and what he termed the empty radicalism of the Third Republic, but for the vulgar cynicism, the bad manners, the corruption and the blackguardism that had fallen on France like a plague. But both his sons were destined for the army, and he himself had achieved some distinction in the Franco-Prussian war. He had finally, at the unanimous insistence of his fellow islanders, accepted the position of mayor of Plessis; but he had only given in after a siege lasting half as long again as that of Troy, and he had always managed, somehow, to avoid donning the tricolor sash. (His first action as mayor had been to design and erect a row of magnificent gasoliers along the arcaded waterfront. Each little quincunx of white glass globes was held aloft by the spiralling and inter-twining tails of five cast-iron dolphins: a measure which, in the eyes of his all proud fellow islanders, con-verted their little capital into the glory of the Antilles.)

Fountains and drinking troughs rose in abundance, Jacobean holidays assumed a new momentum and the life of the island profited by numerous solid benefits to which the Count himself liberally contributed. But his many pictures by Berthe – on horseback, asleep in a rocking-chair with a cigar and a wide hat tipped over his nose, and, once, slightly absurdly, in a tail coat with a Knight of Malta's cross round his neck – depicted someone different from the forbidding traditionalist one might suppose. Page after page revealed a tall handsome man with a forked beard and hair growing thin on top, often in disorder; loose tropical clothes, a flowing lavallière tie and an expression of candid and almost childish good humour. For, when nothing occurred to arouse his political bias, all rancour would deflate and the most transparent benignity would take its place. All his life, indeed, had been devoted to pleasure, and his passion for every kind of sport, his skill at light verses and his mania for amateur theatricals made him the natural centre of the island festivities. He performed competently on half a dozen instruments, on the violin almost with virtuosity. He grasped any pretext for giving holidays to his negroes, often organising and participating in these rustic occasions himself. His kindness and generosity were famous and he was an object of affection, suitably tempered with awe, to the whole population.

The lack of the Serindans' racial intake from their dark fellow islanders was only balanced – through a joyfully conceded survival over many generations, of the ancient *droit de jambage* – by the abundance of their output. The Count's sympathy for the coloured majority during his younger days was solidly proved in his maturity by the features of many of the mulattoes on his estates and in his houses. The paler complexions of these African faces were modified by the unmistakable Serindan stamp – 'of which the most notable sign,' Mademoiselle Berthe observed, 'was the junction of the eyebrows over the bridge of the nose; ce qui donnait un vrai air de famille à toute la maisonnée'. It was rumoured that Gentilien, the grizzled, nearly omnipotent mulatto butler, a man of the Count's age who had served in Bazaine's army in Mexico, was the result of a similar liberal expansiveness of the Count's father, who had been, by all accounts, as well as the largest slave-owner in the island, as passionate a follower of the two veneries as his son. Nothing was ever made explicit but an almost fraternal friendship had united the two men since they were children. The Count frequently expressed his failure to understand the bad terms prevailing between planters and their labourers in less fortunate islands. 'Ils ne savent pas s'y mettre,' he would observe with a shrug. In later years as a married man, his gallantries were restricted to the white race.

It goes without saying that the susceptible Count's heart, in unison with those of most of the masculine creole population of Saint-Jacques, thumped faster at the sudden vision of his beautiful and unknown cousin, and when he, like they, received a kindly but inflexible negative, his disappointment was mitigated by thankfulness for his rescue from a situation which, his natural delicacy may have told him, would have been awkward and undignified. He was quite unaccustomed to his overtures ending thus in the past and his feelings changed to admiration and affection and an almost superstitious awe of Berthe's good sense. She became his confidant and his counsellor on countless matters, and earned the lasting gratitude of the Countess. Madame de Serindan was a beautiful and kind-hearted creature resembling a drawing by Boldini or Helleu. Almost permanently ailing and not particularly clever, she spent much of the year at European watering places. She shared her husband's wonder at Berthe's sagacity. 'They looked on me as a kind of oracle,' Berthe said. Advising the Count about music and horses and the management of his estate – functions for which her upbringing had qualified her in a measure – and the Countess about servants and cooking and dressmaking, became as important a part of her new life as the bringing up of their children.

It was inevitable, too, that the fourteen-years-old Sosthène, in a slightly more articulate fashion than the blind adoration of the other children, should fall in love with her – 'all of which made my task a great deal easier'. (There was nothing boastful about these affirmations. They emerged more by implication as incidental illustrations to other points in her narrative than as direct speech.) Their education at the hands of some local Ursuline sisters and a resident abbé – a very nice man it seemed, but rather an old duffer, whom Madame de

Serindan had summoned, to be tutor to Sosthène, from her parents' house near Vauclin in Martinique – had been adequate but uninspired. M. l'Abbé's chief activity in his old age was saying grace and acting as partner in the games of whist and picquet and bezique which helped to fill the Countess's inexhaustible leisure. His instruction went little further than elementary Latin and the use of globes. Berthe, whose own schooling had been rather of the same kind as her charges, but carried far beyond it by the random and hungry reading of a solitary girl in the country and by a year in Paris, succeeded in changing this considerably. The girls were soon reciting long fragments of Racine and Molière, rattling away at the piano, the harp and the guitar, and drawing and painting and composing with an erratic brilliance that was common to the whole family except the poor Countess.

In Berthe's sketch-books they emerged at first as delightful children, turning, in the years these records covered, into pale beauties with lustrous black hair and large and long-lashed violet eyes. Their natures swung with startling and unpredictable motions from a rather dreamy creole idleness to an excess of animation over which it was difficult even for the capable Berthe to have any control. Everyone else had long since abdicated. Josephine was twelve, Lucienne nine and Solange eight. The youngest of the family, Anne-Jules, who was five when Mademoiselle de Rennes arrived, was the least tractable of all. He would vanish, in spite of threats of punishment, for hours at a time on mysterious expeditions with little negro boys of his own age – errands usually connected with animals, which he had a passion for and a curious knack of taming. Both houses were filled with odd pets. (The most remarkable were a family of manicous, the mother of which carried her dozen young about by twisting her tail parallel to her spine in order that they might loop their own round it and secure their positions on the parent back. A neat sketch demonstrated this performance.) The whole family, including the Count, who was the only one who had lived for any length of time in France, spoke with the queer and charming creole accent – a characteristic derived from the inability of their former slaves to pronounce the letter R. 'It was a pure Incroyable accent,' Berthe explained, 'exactly like that of the dandies of the Directoire.' Again and again I begged her to imitate the Count and the girls talking. 'Ah, Be'the,' she would mimic, 'qu'est qu'on va fai' de ce tewible cheval? C'est un vwai monstwe!' and, 'Ma petite Be'the chéwie, je n'appwendwai jamais la twigonométwie.'

It became plain from the number of drawings, following her slow metamorphosis from a pretty little girl into a ravishing wild-eyed creature of nineteen, that Josephine was the governess's favourite. Berthe did everything she could to conceal her preference. In time this became more than a preference and turned into a passionate friendship, protective and possessive on Berthe's side, romantic, adoring and dependent on Josephine's. Her three years' seniority to the eldest of her sisters in a measure separated her from the other girls, and, as she grew older, with increasing freedom and permission to stay up late, it flung her more completely into the company of Berthe. After Sosthène's departure for France, three years after Berthe's arrival, to study for Saint Cyr (still desperately in love with his beautiful cousin and ex-governess), the two girls were seldom apart. Their friendship flourished by dint of numberless evenings sitting up late in their rooms at the top of the house. (I knew these upper regions well from the sketch-books – the tents of mosquito netting, the crucifix on the wall with its plaited palm-frond, the rosaries lying about, *images d'Epinal* cut out and stuck on the wall, a toy penguin and a couple of dolls superannuated and pensioned off on top of a cupboard; guitars and paint-boxes and the faded bindings of the *Bibliothèque Rose*, the elaborate West Indian dressing-tables, the upheaval of tree-tops under the windows.) Their intimacy was fostered by long rides through the waving avenues of sugar-cane and the nocturnal highwoods alive with fireflies. It was the world of *Paul et Virginie*: dark forests and sweeping savannahs, hot noondays and shadowy valleys between the mornes[1] and silver nights when the bamboos showered their silent expanding fountains towards the moon. Everything that an idyll possesses that is most primitive and innocent seemed to surround these girls, like a Garden of Eden on the volcano's side. The Atlantic storms pounded to windward beyond the watershed,

1. West Indian volcanic hills.

but the demesne of Beauséjour sloped peacefully between tree-feathered canefield and parkland. It was bounded by mountains and by ravines where the distant cascades fell through the gloom of the forest like shining horse-tails. Its western boundary was the calm leeward shore and the smooth sweep of the Caribbean Sea. Scattered across that blue expanse, the Desirade, Marie Galante and the little archipelago of the Saints trailed north and west. The horizon where the sun burnt itself out among the monumental clouds like a phoenix's funeral that was resolemnised each evening stretched from the towering cloud-smothered Souffrière of Guadeloupe to the phantom spire of Morne Diablotin in Dominica. For Berthe and Josephine it was a miraculous region suspended in space, where everything – the forests, the sea, the air and the sunset – united in a favourable conspiracy. 'All this may sound a bit silly,' Mademoiselle Berthe suddenly broke off, 'but it was the happiest time of my life. I asked nothing more than for it to go on for ever.'

*　　　*　　　*

It did, almost. For as long, that is, as anything was allowed to continue in Saint-Jacques. But, a few weeks before the ball in which all the island affairs culminated, something went wrong. This was in the early years of the present century. Berthe was twenty-four and Josephine eighteen. Relations between the creole squire-archy and the government administration from France, never very cordial, had been growing steadily worse. It had not been too bad in the past, for the Governor and his staff had been content to take the advice of the creoles on most matters; and, as Saint-Jacques, unlike many of the Antilles, had long been famous for the harmony of its internal affairs, all had gone well. But two years ago a new Governor, called Valentin Sciocca, and an entirely new staff, had been appointed. It was the time when Waldeck-Rousseau and Combes were the most prominent figures in French politics, the era of the Expulsion of the Congregations and the *Affaire des Fiches*; and Sciocca, an affluent professional politician of Corsican origin – formerly implicated, it was rumoured, in several shady affairs – was all that was most unacceptable to the Royalist and profoundly Catholic creoles: a radical, an anti-clerical, an atheist, a suspected freemason and an open Dreyfusard. ('He was right on the last point of course, as all the world knows,' said Berthe, 'and the Jacobeans were wrong. But feelings ran very high at the time.') His manner and his general vulgarity, it appeared, were as disagreeable to the creoles as his political associations. What was perhaps stranger at first glance was his lack of success with the negro population. A herald of reform and a noisy demagogue at every chance he could find for a public speech, he was politely clapped each time, but frustrated in the implementation of his measures by obstructiveness among the black officials and among the labourers themselves. He was maddened at every turn by the reiteration of 'fô dimandé ça à Messié le Comte'. As the popular mayor of Plessis, the Count's position was strong. As head of the creoles and a figure beloved by the whole island, it was invincible. He availed himself of it with savage delight, rubbing his hands at each fresh reverse of 'ces cwapules de métwopolitains'. Sciocca he never referred to except as 'cet animal corse'. It was the most exciting and satisfactory sport with which he had yet experimented and the administration of the island was soon at a standstill.

'The pity,' Berthe went on, 'was that Sciocca wasn't a bad fellow really. But he had the manners of a cab-driver and less tact than a boot.' The whole island began to suffer from this deadlock and soon the administrative body and the creoles themselves began to wish with equal fervour that the feud between the Count and the Governor would end. Something had to be done. 'It was patched up in the end,' Berthe continued, 'partly by me, partly by the Captain.

'Haven't I told you about the Captain?' She turned the pages of a sketch-book and handed it across to me. 'There you are: *Henri Joubert, capitaine de fregate en retraite, Beauséjour, 1898* – the year he settled in Saint-Jacques. He was a well-known writer and poet, though few people read him now. He specialised in outlandish settings – islands, deserts, pagodas, icebergs and so on, in a most melodramatic style. I don't expect you have ever come across any of his books – *Dans le Bled, Aurore Boréale Crépuscule du Bosphore, Chandernagore* and *Les Tonkinoises*. I never cared for them much, but we were all very fond of the Captain himself.'

It was a very detailed sketch. The author's face, one eyesocket expanded with a ribboned eyeglass, gazed deep-eyed from the page. The hair, parted in the middle, swept away in two curling wings and a little moustache was twisted up musketeerishly above a mouth with many curves whose benignity and humour belied the bristly overshadowing challenge. One hand, emerging from a stiff striped cuff fastened with large cameo links, trailed, limp and gloved, over a rakishly crooked knee; a long quill pen flourished from fore-finger and thumb. The other elbow rested on an African drum. The fore-arm rose perpendicular, and the hand, the gloved ring-finger of which was adorned with a heavy signet, was twisted outwards and palm upwards, holding a thick cigarette in a foppish gesture.

'Poor Captain!' Berthe said. 'He was charming, but in some ways rather absurd. He lived in a little house in the negro quarter, surrounded by gongs and incense burners and nargilehs and a host of young negro servants that he called "my bronze and ebony Apollos". They said he smoked opium and he was sometimes known as *le parfumeur* because of the cloud of exotic scents that always followed him about; and his grey hair was dyed a deep chestnut. He had a *fin de siècle* style that one rarely meets nowadays.' Berthe laughed. 'He was very kind and everybody liked him, the Count especially – he was such a diverting companion and such an in-ventive collaborator in the conduct of *fêtes*.'

The Captain was a brilliant storyteller, as inexhaus-tible as a circumnavigator, and the family would listen to him with the raptness of a Renaissance court. After dinner on the terrace at Beauséjour he would entertain the Serindans for hours with tales of his far-flung adventures on the pampas, in Papua, on the Siberian tundras or in Madagascar at the court of Queen Ranavalo. His anecdotes of literary colleagues and high life and the stage, and his imitations of Castellane and Montesquieu, of Sarah Bernhardt and Réjane and Eleanore Duse and of Coquelin and Mounet-Sully would set the Count mopping the tears of laughter from his cheek with a large bandana handkerchief. He was an ardent bicyclist, he had been for a ride in an automobile and had even made an ascent in a balloon, the story of which the Count never tired of hearing. (How well the Captain told it! The crowd in the Champ de Mars as the great globe, striped in segments of silver and scarlet, floated up and above the Eiffel Tower, down the Seine, over the chimerae and the flying buttresses of Notre Dame and the fields and villages of the Ile de France. . . . The conversations with the literary critic and the two actresses from the *Varietés* that were with him in the basket, the muddles with the sandbags and the anchor, the champagne corks popping in mid-air as Chantilly floated underneath. . . . The silence except for the astonished twittering of thousands of birds a few yards below in the tree-tops of the Forest of Compiègne; and, at last, the dispersal of a great dappled troop of fallow deer that watched them in a ring from the surrounding beech-trees as they settled among the swans in the middle of a lake . . .)

But he was also – and in this dual function the Captain was unique in Saint-Jacques – a favourite at Government House. Berthe had for some time been exhorting the Count on the folly of his feud with Sciocca and when she enrolled the Captain in her support ('Come, come my dear Agénor, you are driving the poor man mad'), the Count gradually began to give way; the more easily as his unbroken string of victories was beginning to rob the conflict of its zest. Also, perhaps, because Madame Sciocca, a flamboyant creature from Marseilles for whom the Count had invented, without a shred of ascertainable foundation, raffish origins on the waterfront of her native town, was by no means ill-looking. The Captain tactfully proposed that, as a magnanimous gesture of forgiveness, Sciocca and his staff should be invited, for the first time since their arrival, to the Serindans' Shrove Tuesday ball, the apex of the Jacobean carnival and the great social function of the year. The Count's united eyebrows descended in a spasm of disgust and his beard and moustache bristled like the spines of a hedgehog.

'What? Ask that animal into the house with all his Jacobin scum?'

The Captain stood up. 'My dear friend,' he sighed wearily, 'if you were a modern Italian living in Rome instead of a Frenchman in the Caribbean, I really believe your whole life would be spent plotting the return of the Tarquins.'

The Count laughed and then, with one of those sudden changes for which he was well known, he threw his hands negligently into the air and exclaimed, 'Enfin! Qu'ils viennent! We can always have the house spring-cleaned next day. . . .'

'Agénor,' the Captain murmured, as his gloved hand descended lightly for a moment on his host's forearm, 'you are goodness in human form.' Picking up his straw boater before another change could occur he sailed away like a dove returning to the ark with an olive twig locked in its beak.

Meanwhile, in the private world of Berthe and Josephine, all had not been well. Towards the end of January, Berthe fell sick with an attack of malaria which kept her bedridden for a month. During most of this time Josephine would keep her company; re-arranging her pillows, sitting by her bed, and, when Berthe was capable of listening, reading aloud. But the younger girl, who was never able to stay indoors for long, would absent herself on long rides, solitary ones now, returning later and later in the evening. As the severity of the disease abated, Berthe thought she noticed that Josephine came back from these lonely expeditions in a state of elation she found difficult to conceal. One evening she rushed into Berthe's room with shining eyes, threw her hat and whip on the sofa and then, scrambling inside the mosquito net, flung herself flat on Berthe's bed. Leaning on the pillow, she propped her chin in her hands. After gazing wildly at the invalid for a few seconds, she said, 'Darling Berthe, I've got a great secret to tell you', and then, after a pause, 'I've fallen in love.' Berthe succeeded in hiding the sudden stab of anguish that transfixed her, and, forcing a smile, said, 'I thought something had happened. Please tell me.'

Josephine, it seems, had met this new figure, also on horseback, by chance, on the second of her lonely rides, behind the canefields of Savanne de Rohan in the foot-hills of the Salpetrière. Since then they had met every afternoon; declared their love, kissed, sworn to marry. 'I knew something of the kind was bound to happen,' Berthe said meditatively, 'and assumed he must be the young La Tour d'Astirac of Savanne, or one of the Tharonnes of Morne Zombi, the estate beyond; perfectly eligible and proper after all, distant relations of the Serindans and admirable matches. Tiresomely, Josephine refused for a long time to tell me his name.'

At last, hiding her anxiety, and after endless teasing and coaxing, Berthe managed to extort a conditional answer. 'I'll tell you, Berthe darling, if you promise to keep it a secret.'

'I promise.'

'Well,' Josephine said hesitantly, 'it's Marcel Sciocca, the Governor's son.'

Berthe jerked bolt upright in bed. 'Josephine!' she exclaimed, 'I hope this is a joke.'

'By the terror of the girl's expression,' Berthe said, 'I must have looked as if I were about to lay hands on her. I managed to control my anger and soon understood that it was far from being a joke. "But Josephine," I kept asking her, "how could it be Sciocca?" For, if his father was perhaps not so bad as he was painted, his son was horrible. He combined the appearance of a

Neapolitan barber with the manner of a prize bounder and the reputation of a crook; all of which I didn't hesitate to tell her. But no, she insisted, that was all prejudice and part of her papa's political hobby-horse. This was odd language for her to use. She was passionately devoted to the Count. I told her as well, in the conventional way, that it would kill her father should he ever hear of it. I didn't mention my own savage feelings of jealousy in the matter but I made her promise not to see him again. It all ended in floods of tears until at last she fell asleep.'

During the following weeks of Berthe's convalescence, Josephine was seldom far from her side, and everything, except for long abstracted silences on Josephine's part and a terrible anxiety on Berthe's, seemed as it had been before. Their ideas were suddenly changed by the joyful event of Sosthène's arrival from Saint Cyr, where he had had a stormy but not altogether unsuccessful career. He was due to return soon for a course at Saumur before joining a regiment of hussars. He came back with Madame de Serindan, who had been spending the winter between Paris and Contrexéville. Sosthène seemed more deeply than ever in love with Berthe, and she was submitted to an impassioned fusillade of proposals and, alternatively, to threats of suicide. Sosthène looked younger than his age and his character was an odd and contradictory mixture of youthfulness and extreme precocity. It was plain that his ardour was no longer to be stemmed, as it had been before his departure, by telling him not to be a Silly Billy. If Berthe had consented, the Serindans would have been delighted at the match, in spite of the four years difference in age. 'But it was out of the question,' Berthe concluded. 'How ridiculous and rather pathetic it all seems now, and what a long time ago. . . .'

*　　　*　　　*

Mademoiselle de Rennes had to leave for Athens on some business or other and she was away almost a week. One evening Phrosoula appeared at my little hotel with a note from Berthe asking me to dinner.

There was a full moon and the table was laid among olive trees beside an old well that plunged deep into the rock. The water was brought to the top by a windlass, ice cold after long winding. Phrosoula rested her tray on the edge of the well-head and leant against it while she waited to change the plates. Berthe talked about Athens and the incidents that had occurred on the steamer to and fro.

When we had drunk our coffee, the girl put a full pitcher of wine on the table between our wicker chairs, said goodnight and vanished. The olives advanced to the brink of the headland, each ancient stem twisting in a contrary direction to its neighbour. Many of the trees were so old that the trunks were split wide apart to the roots, each half following the spiral convolutions of the other, like dancing-partners in a waltzing forest; the rising moon, entangled overhead in the silver and lanceolate leaves, had frozen these gyrations into immobility. This highly literary simile was Berthe's, and a complementary arabesque of her glowing cigarette end underlined the verve of this imaginary choreography. The cue seemed apt, so, 'Berthe,' I ventured, 'I wish you would tell me about the Ball'.

'A – ha,' she said with a sigh, 'the Ball ...' The orange cigarette-end came to rest on the arm of the chair and after a few moments of silence we were back in Saint-Jacques on the last day of carnival in the first decade of the twentieth century.

*   *   *

I knew the appearance and the atmosphere of the Serindan house in Plessis so well from Berthe's discourse and her innumerable sketches that it was as

though I had been present at the preparations for the Shrove Tuesday Ball she so evocatively described: the great white rooms opening to each other through fluted Corinthian pillars of wood; the crowding, rather primitive portraits of dead Serindans in wigs, or later, in high collars, by Clamart the student of Liotard; the plaster flourishes and rococo cartwheels of foliage on the ceilings; the chandeliers with their prismatic and melodiously jangling lustres, all of them bright now with innumerable candles, and already the meeting place of an army of little moths, which, in advance of the guests, had fluttered in from the forest.

The Serindan house was not only the biggest in Plessis, but the highest perched. It was islanded among ascending and descending terraces, and the balustrades were adorned with posturing graces and marble nymphs. Beyond their elegant barrier, the forest began: a huge wilderness of tangled ceibas and balisiers and tree-ferns that only halted a slanting six miles beyond at the jagged crater of the Salpetrière. The day had ended in a flaunting sunset so apocalyptic – a Last Judgement, an apotheosis, an assumption, one could have thought – that each falling ray seemed a ladder for the descending Paraclete, and Berthe almost expected to see long-shafted trumpets advance along the slanting beams from the gold and crimson clouds. Then it suddenly died away into night. The volcano had been burning for the last week or so with unaccustomed vigour. Now it hung in the dark like a bright red torch, prompting the island wiseacres, mindful of the terrible eruptions that had

coincided over a century ago with the fall of the Bastille,
to shake their heads. But such renewals of activity and
such gloomy presages recurred every few years. Each
minor overflow of lava, heralded invariably by showers
of ashes and an overpowering heat, was always halted
by those intervening canyons known as *les chaudières* – a
grey desert region of fumeroles and volcanic gas and
half fossilised trees. 'Ga'dez Salpetwière!" the negroes
said joyfully to each other; 'li pas faché, li fait bomba
pou' Ma'di Gwas, comme nous', and the carnival drums
beat vigorously all over the town. There had been not
a drop of rain for many days – a rare event even in this
dry season – and the trade winds had ceased altogether.
The heat was appalling.

But nothing could repress the Count's enthusiasm on
such an occasion. (The Countess, ensconced in a
rocking-chair, gently fanning herself in a cool little
room with a pretty Clamart pastoral scene on the
ceiling, had long ago resigned from such duties.
Lavender- and barley-water and hartshorn stood ready
on a little table. Safely embowered there among indoor
shrubs, she turned the pages of *La Mode à Paris*.)
He and the Captain and Berthe were directing the
decoration of the two great saloons where the dancing
would take place. Negroes had been at work all day
plaiting thick festoons of bougainvillea and poinsettia,
and when the Captain arrived, the Count, Berthe and
Gentilien, with the children and an army of servants,
were looping them from the walls to the chandeliers.
The Captain's hands had gone up in horror.

'Agénor! Berthe! Gentilien! It's hideous! Pray throw those monstrosities away at once, it's worse than an English Christmas at Cape Town. Nothing but hibiscus and magnolia, I beg!'

The Count was only downcast for a moment and the work had to begin all over again. The new decorations were ready just in time. 'No, *not* strung from the chandeliers but like this,' the Captain insisted, 'hanging in swags from the cornice and twisted in spirals round the curtains and the pillars.'

The result was charming. The heavy scent of the garlands mingled with that of polish and beeswax. Together they arranged the great sheaves of flowers and chose the places for the branching candelabra. (Each candle was enclosed in the swelling and waisted cylinder of a glittering hurricane glass.) Next they inspected the cold table, with its hams and its quails in aspic, the giant lobsters and crabs, the ivory pyramids of *chou coco* and *chou palmiste* for each one of which a tall palm tree had been felled in order that the precious heart might be dislodged; the mounds of soursops and mangos, the pineapples and sapodillas and sweetsops and granadillas and avocado pears; the cold barracks for champagne, where on banks of ice from Nova Scotia, the magnums of Aï reclined in green and gold battalions; the arrays of rum and syrup jugs, the lemons and the nutmeg and the newly-cut yard-long swizzle sticks for the *punch martiniquais*; the ingredients for the sorbets and the Sangaree were methodically laid out along a dresser. At noon the Count and Gentilien had descended the spiral to the cellars with the gravity of turnkeys, reascending from the cobwebbed catacombs (which warrened the volcanic rock on which the house was built), like chaplains hearing a succession of fragile and wonder-working reliquaries. Now the count gazed with the tenderness of a nurse at the alcove where, like sleeping children who must come to no harm, the fabulous clarets, uncorked with almost alchemical skill, lay at rest; cradled there for the last few hours, sleepers of Ephesus all gently waking, they mingled with the Antillean air the quiet breath they had held since their infancy by far-off castles on the banks of the Garonne.

In the kitchen, urchins, sea-eggs and dwarf oysters – the last still clustering in scores on lengths of mangrove-stalk – were heaped in pails. The snow-white whorls of the conch shells (each of them opening to display a pink internal helix) were arrayed like a tritons' orchestra announcing, in a silent fanfare, the later delights of *lambi flambé au rhum*. A swarm of little frogs swam agitatedly round their tank; the great shell of a turtle had already been evacuated by its lodger. Horny backed iguanas, trussed like captured dragons, moved restlessly in their baskets. The Count stopped and gazed at them.

'What beautiful and mythical creatures!' he apostrophised. 'To think that our pygmy ancestors trembled before their giant ancestors in prehistoric times!' He picked one up. Its tail swayed in uneasy protest. 'And now, poor creatures, how the rôles are reversed!' Stooping, he whistled a few bars from the overture to *Lucia di Lammermoor*, and soon the dragon was motionless, as though these notes had mesmerized it into an aesthetic trance. Running his finger along its jagged backbone to the tip of the slender striped tail, he replaced it with a sigh. 'They love Donizetti,' he said; then, with a slight change of key, turning to the Captain: 'I've discovered a new way of cooking them, Henri. Don't forget to tell me what you think of it. . . .' Outside under the mango trees a dozen negroes turned spits on which sucking pigs were impaled over trenches of charcoal. White teeth were bared in greeting among the shadows. 'Goutez ça, Messié le Comte,' said one of the negroes, snipping off a crisp ear. 'Ou ka volé au pawadis!'

They returned munching to the hall, where the servants were waiting. The Count always dressed them for this dance in the liveries of his great-grandfather's time, which had been preserved in great chests in the attics. Many of them, drawn by Berthe, were familiar figures: Charlemagne, Gratien, Mignon, Ajax, Fortuné, Hyacinthe, Zénon, Félix, Théodule, Sarpedon, Numa Pompilius, Siriaque, Clovis, and Hiram Abif, a rather secretive young man formerly apprenticed to a brick-layer; and a dozen more. They were dressed in white breeches with a bunch of ribbons at the knee, and their feet and legs were bare. Their white linen shirts had billowing sleeves and ribbons at the collar and the cuff. Broad yellow sashes bound their middles, and their torsos were enclosed in black plush boleros galooned with gold lace. They wore golden

ear-rings and large black and yellow turbans fastened
with plumes, and round their necks hung silver plaques
on chains incised with the Serindan cognizance: a shield
bearing three greyhounds passant on a bend on a field
of cross-crosslets within a tressure flory-counter-flory.

Then the girls – Dody, Uldarix, Modestine, Lucette,
Baby, La Grande Suzanne, Vénus, Eulalie, Marie Médicis,
Léocade, Scholastique, Jug Betty and Joan from Antigua,
Bibiane and a swarm of others – lined up giggling.
Berthe and Gentilien – the latter dressed in buckled shoes
and a black and gold frock coat with epaulettes and
aiguillettes, his grizzled hair redundantly powdered –
straightened the tall cylindrical turbans of the girls and
the huge yellow and black bows down the front; puffed
out a pannier here, tightened a sash there, and smoothed
the pleated skirts over their bare feet. The Count
beamed, exclaiming, 'Charmant mes enfants!' – a
familiar mode of address which in three cases and
possibly more, was literally exact in this instance – then
clapped his hands, and the girls scuttled off laughing.
But the orchestra, assembled and trained by himself at
Beauséjour and transported to Plessis for the Carnival,
was his favourite care. He had sent for the sheet music of
the most recent dance tunes from Paris, and, sitting at
the piano, seizing now a violin, now a 'cello, he went
over the difficult passages till all seemed perfect.

'Now, Henri,' he said to the Captain, 'it's time to
change. And, I entreat you, please be here when your
Metropolitan friends arrive. We shall all be lost without
you.'

The Captain shouted from the doorstep that he would rather be late for the Field of the Cloth of Gold.

* * *

Upstairs in the girls' rooms, all was at sixes and sevens. A flotsam of stockings, petticoats, cardboard boxes and tissue-paper smothered the beds and overflowed to the floor. Gentilien's wife, the old and bulky Fanette, who had been the *Da*, or Nanny, of the Serindan children since they were born, presided over half a dozen maids who knelt round the four girls with their mouths full of pins: taking in last-minute tucks, arranging ribbons, brushing and braiding hair. The Count had given all four of them new dresses for the ball. Berthe's was green – 'they thought it went best with my fair hair' – Lucienne's pale blue, and Solange's pink. Josephine ran into Berthe's room, pirouetted on one white satin toe with a swirl of skirts and then stood still with a look of expectancy. It was her first low dress, a stiff pagoda of white taffeta that made the warm olive skin of her shoulders, and the dusky smoothness of her cheek, shine with the lustre of ivory on silver, and burn with the utmost fervour of créole beauty: a warmth accentuated by the pallor of the gardenias along the corsage of her dress and the three gardenias in her blue-black hair.

'O, Josephine,' Berthe could not help saying. 'How lovely you look!'

'Do I, darling Berthe?' she answered in a gasp. 'And you?' They held each other at arms' length.

'Josephine had been very excited all day,' Berthe

explained to me, 'and I hoped she had forgotten all about her romance with M. Sciocca. She was the giddiest of the three girls and excitement at the prospect of the ball and her new dress easily accounted for her exaltation. But I could not forget that he would be there with his father, and decided to keep my eyes open.

'While we were gazing at each other in admiration, Anne-Jules burst into the room. "You girls may think you're something," he shouted, "but you wait. I've got a surprise in here," he pointed to a mysterious basket, "that's going to wake everybody up!" He had been more than usually hard to find during the last week, always returning from the woods late for meals, and invariably in the company of a little black boy of his own age, Gentilian's son, Pierrot – though Anne-Jules did not know it, his own first cousin – who now hovered in the background. The other girls came running in and the boys disappeared. They were joined by Sosthène, who emerged from his room looking tall and grave in a brand new uniform. After suitable exclamations, we joined hands and rustled down the great staircase, all feeling very proud of ourselves. Modestine, Josephine's maid, ran halfway down to give Josephine a fan that she had forgotten. We were only just in time, for the first guests were arriving as we reached the hall.'

The first arrivals were cousins and neighbours: the entire vast family of La Tour d'Astirac-Belcastel of Savanne de Rohan. They streamed into the hall with kisses and exclamations of wonder at the dresses and the flowers. After that, the carriages rolled up one after the other, till the courtyard was ringing with trampling and spark-striking hooves. Wheels ground and squeaked on the flagstones. Many kinds of vehicles appeared – modern barouches and victorias, neat flies and coupés, antiquated berlines and *bourbonnaises* and here and there a smart turnout *à la Daumont* – each unloading at the Count's staircase the denizens of all the *gentilhommières* of Saint-Jacques. With shouts and cracking whips the equipages moved on. The newly alighted groups flowed indoors between two gigantic stone figures of Atlas which stooped with frowning brows and contorted biceps beneath a massive pediment loaded with blazons and cornucopias hewn out of coral rock. (In the heart of the petrified cascades of fruits and flowers that overflowed the plinth, single-horned supporters with tempestuous manes hoisted a great stone shield on which, beneath a nine-pearled circlet, a baton in bend sinister debruised the du Plessis canton quartering the hounds of Serindan, and an inescutcheon with the rose of Fontenay was superimposed in pretence.)

I made Berthe repeat the picturesque names as though she were fulfilling Gentilian's rôle of butler: the Solignacs of Triste Etang, the Vauduns of Anse Verte, the Tharonnes of Morne Zombi, the Vertprés of Battaka and Bombardopolis, the Chaumes of Carbet du Roi, the Cussacs of Ajoupa, the Rivrys of Allégresse, the O'Rourkes of Bouillante, the Kerascoët-Plougastels of Cayes Fendus, the Fains of Noé des Bois, the La Mottes of Piton-Noir, the Fertés of Deux Rivières, the La

Flour d'Aiguesamares of Sans Pitié, the Montgirards of Morne Bataille, the Chambines de la Forest d'Ivry of Pointe d'Ivry and the La Popelinières from the strangely named acres of Confiture; Hucs, Dentus, Pornics, Médards, Vamels; here and there a visiting cousin from another island – a de Jaham or a Despointes from Martinique, a du Boulay from English St Lucia. A few prominent members of the little Jewish community of Plessis – names like Spinoza, Leon, da Costa, Astrologo and da Cordova – arrived together. These were the descendants of Sephardic families that had fled from Ferdinand and Isabella to the Brazilian town of Pernambuco; taking refuge, when the town was captured, in the hospitable Antilles. Most of the sugar- and rum- and molasses-brokerage in Saint-Jacques was in their hands, and they had occupied for generations an honourable position in the island.

The Captain's arrival was greeted with acclamation, for – 'with his cheeks a little pinker than usual,' Berthe said, 'and his eye-brows a little more poignantly dark' – he came swaying along in a painted Sedan chair upholstered in purple satin and borne by two of his dark retinue. He swore that the streets where he lived were too narrow for any larger equipage. Alighting with the resilience of an aeronaut, he coiled towards the Count and Countess, and stooped over her hand with a delicate interweaving of compliments. The effluvia of oriental essences surrounded him. His hair had been brushed and cajoled into an ambrosial nest, his moustache was crisply tonged, and the hand that held the flattened opera hat against his erect and pigeon-breasted torso was gloved in lilac. Screwing in his eyeglass, he peered challengingly round the room with an air of debonair severity, epitomising, his attitude seemed to say, the fourfold essence of mariner, explorer, man of letters and balloonist.

The band and the Count's tunes from Paris were a quick success; the floor soon filled with couples, and the intervals were loud with the planters' deep voices and the fluttering and light-hearted tones of their wives and daughters, as bright, all of them, and as lively as humming birds. The strange creole diction, whose oddity and charm in Berthe's ears still survived its six years' familiarity, twittered in the warm candle-lit air. The brilliant dresses of the women were flanked by the high collars and stiff round plastrons, the white clothes and the scarlet sashes of the men. Negroes in their black and gold liveries skimmed among the guests, holding great silver trays laden with champagne glasses or long goblets of Martinique punch high above their turbans. A violet splash betokened the presence of the Bishop of Plessis, deep in colloquy with a dowager from the other side of the island. Every time the music stopped, the sounds of carnival from the rest of Plessis sailed in through the windows.

'Son Excellence le Gouverneur,' Gentilien announced in one of these pauses, 'et Madame Sciocca.' The Count, with the Countess rustling beside him in the new Worth dress she had brought back from Paris, moved to meet them. The august visitors appeared in the doorway.

The Governor was a stocky figure in a black evening coat. A broad red ribbon ran across his shirt front and he wore a heavy black moustache, a fringe and pince-nez. Standing hesitantly between the Corinthian columns, he mopped the back of his neck with a silk handkerchief. Madame Sciocca quite over-shadowed him. She was a tall and opulent woman with a mass of red hair. Her towering coiffure was crowned with a high mauve aigrette that matched the mauve sequins of her dress and also her long mauve gloves, round one wrist of which a heavy pearl necklace was twisted; a large ostrich feather fan fluttered up and down as languorously as the flabella that once cooled the brow of the Egyptian queen. The Captain, presiding in the midst of the newly-formed group by the door, tactfully abetted the meeting of the Creoles with the gubernatorial couple and the sombre looking staff attending them. The group moved slowly across the floor to a table by the largest window.

'Madame,' the Governor said feelingly, offering one arm to the timid Countess, and mopping his brow, 'quelle épouvantable chaleur!' The Count's natural affability was never more apparent. Madame Sciocca rested her hand on his gallantly crooked elbow, and gazed round the room. 'Mais quelle splendeur chez vous, mon cher comte,' she sighed, and her eyelids seemed to move with the same torpid voluptuousness as the long white feathers of her fan. 'C'est une vraie splendeur. . . .' The Count's eyes, glancing down at the thick white throat and the monumental curves at his side and catching the glint of the two green eyes now swivelling towards his own, were focused in expert appraisal that soon kindled into a bright answering spark of approbation.

A quarter of an hour later, when the party was safely established, Berthe was standing in one of the window recesses talking to the Captain. 'Thank God!' he murmured in her ear, 'I believe everything is going like a honeymoon.' He looked down with satisfaction at the outstretched lilac fingers of one of his hands and smoothed an imaginary wrinkle on the little finger. 'I wonder who told *la belle dame Sciocca* about my new gloves – not that I mind, my dear – far from it. Plagiary is really very flattering. . . .'

The Count by now was waltzing gaily round and round with Madame Sciocca. Nimbly reversing towards Berthe and her companion, his revolutions brought him and his partner close to the alcove. The Count smiled at Berthe over his partner's shoulder, and she thought she could catch the ghost of a wink in his jovial face. She burst out laughing and said to the Captain, 'I believe you are right'. The Captain placed his hand on his shirt front and rolling his eyes histrionically, said, 'C'est Vénus toute entière à sa proie attachée!' and, delighted that all was going so well, went off to assist Madame de Serindan with the Governor.

M. Marcel Sciocca – the Governor's son by an earlier marriage that had been dissolved by divorce (it was rumoured in whispers), in order to make way for the present Madame Sciocca – sat on the Countess's other side, fluently reinforcing his father's rather cumbrous devoirs with a florid battery of compliments. 'He was a tall, blue-chinned brute of about forty,' Berthe said, 'with a pale fleshy face smothered in rice powder, a deep and modulated voice, an oily address and a permanent flashing smile whose total emptiness was only diversified by half a dozen gold teeth – a dancing master beginning to run to fat, and rigged out in huge diamond studs. He was, in fact, so much a caricature of the ideal *rastaquouère* that Josephine's former infatuation became every minute more difficult to understand. But I was relieved to see that not only did he not ask Josephine to dance, but not a glance was exchanged between them. Josephine had taken refuge at the other end of the room, dancing entirely with her cousins and several times running with Hubert de la Tour, the young man whom the parents on both sides had in mind as Josephine's future husband. I heaved a sigh of relief. The dance came to an end and Cousin Agénor led Madame Sciocca back to his table.'

The floor was bare. But, before the dancers could disperse to the lantern-lit terraces – the heat seemed to be growing more oppressive every minute – they were arrested by a shrill cry from the head of the stairs: 'Please wait a moment, everybody!'

It was Anne-Jules, standing on the landing with Pierrot at his side. They were dressed from head to foot in palm-leaves, and wore tall gold necromancer's hats painted with a pattern of stars and planets and snakes. They advanced to the head of the stairs, turned back to back with a precision that must have been often rehearsed and slid down opposite banisters which deposited them simultaneously on the empty dance-floor. Advancing to the middle, Pierrot placed a foot-stool under the central chandelier, and on top of this Anne-Jules placed his mysterious basket. Then, bowing towards his father's table, he said, 'Vos Excellences, Monsieur le comte, madame la comtesse, messieurs, mesdames, mesdemoiselles, nous allons vous wévéler le woi du Carnaval.' Bending to the square basket, he opened a trap door in the side and intoned the following words:

> Beauté supwême et toute puissante,
> et majesté du carnaval,
> Dans les tenèbwes languissantes,
> Sors du palais, diwige le bal!

Both boys then began a low, soft coaxing whistle and, in a stage whisper, said in unison, 'Sors, Sardanapale!' The long drawn whistling continued, and the guests craned forward with a flutter of curiosity. 'Sors, Sardanapale!', Anne-Jules and Pierrot repeated, and a dark object appeared from the little wicker door. It moved from side to side for a few seconds, curled downwards to the floor, and then, followed by two flowing yards of scaly and noiseless sinuosity as thick as a wrist, began to move across the parquet. There was a general gasp and one or two half-suppressed screams. Following it, Anne-Jules changed his whistle to a succession of staccato notes and the snake raised its head high in the air. Its head was followed by an erect pillar of trunk which stretched every second longer until its entire length, rising from and balancing on a small terminal circle of tail, seemed to be standing perpendicular. The terrible triangular and horny head, lowered at right angles to its trunk, swayed from side to side with a drunken-seeming motion. A forked tongue darted swiftly in and out of hissing jaws.

A shock of terror at the sight of the *fer de lance*, poised in the classical posture preparatory to striking, ran through the room like a wave of electricity. The bite of the trigonocephalus brings certain death within the hour. In a sudden scurry the dancers crowded back from the possible ambit of its leap. The Count was the first to break the silence.

'Anne-Jules,' he shouted, 'do you know how to make that brute get back into the basket?'

Anne-Jules looked at his father round-eyed with feigned surprise. 'Yes, papa.'

'Then do so directly.'

Still softly whistling, he approached the poised serpent from behind, caught hold of the back of the hissing head, then, lifting it in the air, gathered up the heavy slack with his other hand and walked to where Pierrot was holding the basket open. Everyone held their breath. The Countess, white as chalk, was feverishly fingering her châtelaine. Anne-Jules dropped the tail through the trap-door and coiled the long body after it until only the head remained outside. With a murmur of 'rentre, Sardanapale,' he dropped it inside and Pierrot closed the lid.

There was a universal escape of breath and a slightly

hysterical rush of talk. The Count strode to the basket, picked it up and handed it to Gentilien, whose pupils were revolving in apprehensive circles of white.

'Take this brute away and destroy it. And you,' he said severely, turning to Anne-Jules, 'go straight up to bed and stay there!'

The two little wizards, their conical hats hanging dejectedly now, made for the stairs and, climbing sadly to the landing, vanished.

'I apologise for my son's ridiculous behaviour,' the Count said, with a circular gesture to his guests, and then waved to the band. Raggedly at first they struck up a polka. He seized Berthe round the waist and off they galloped, the musicians recovering the beat once more from their master's determined pacings. Other couples joined them and soon, in a hubbub of chatter, the Ball revived.

Exactly at the right moment a diversion reinforced the Count's efforts. It was the custom of the Shrove Tuesday masques in Saint-Jacques to range through the town, holding the burghers to ransom in the streets with mock threats, and entering their houses, where a libation of rum was claimed as a prerogative, and willingly granted. This was the sort of thing the Count loved and the masques could always rely on a generous reception at his house. The sounds of carnival had been growing steadily louder. Now, a score of negroes, dressed in fluttering rags designed to resemble grave-cloths and their faces painted like skulls, burst into the ballroom with savage yells, waving flaming torches over their heads. They advanced across the floor where a passage opened in front of them, passed out of the windows to leave their torches on the terrace and returned across the ballroom to usher in their companions. And in they came. Some of them wore torn frock coats and battered top hats. Others were dressed in the scarlet rags and the long noses, the painted ears and the horns, of devils. There were mock aristocrats in powdered wigs, and these were followed by beautiful negresses and quadroons and octaroons and *capresses* dressed in all the splendour of the *gwan' wobe*, the *foulard*, the *gwains d'or* and the *madwas* – the tight marmalade coloured turbans with the ends tied in three jutting spikes that signified, for those who understood the sign language, amorous complaisance to all-comers. (Some of the largest of these – towering *mamelouques* and *sacatras* and *griffonnes* – were really men in disguise.) Scarlet and saffron and black were the predominating colours, and many of the girls had crimson hearts painted on their cheeks. All were masked. Recognisable under their disguises, and beautifully rigged out in feathers and great paste jewels, were some of the leading mulatto *matadores* – the Jacobean equivalent of *poules de luxe* – drawn from their gilded ease into this plebeian swarm by an unconquerable desire to see the inside of the Serindan house.

(A number of the creole squires, Berthe noticed, and some of the Governor's staff, at once retreated to strategic positions behind pillars where they might escape immediate recognition. . . .)

Half a dozen black dominoes were scattered among the rest. Human bats came beating in with large ribbed wings, pursued by leopards and tigers and jaguars whose faces were covered by the animals' masks, while the skins flew loose behind them. Round their waists were kilts of sugar-cane and balisier. Mummers riding paper horses and hippopotamuses and dragons and giraffes, all vividly caparisoned, came prancing and rearing after them. Their steeds were built out on hoops round their waists, and dummy human legs sat astride them in saddles and stirrups. The riders' real legs and the four putative ones of their mounts were concealed by gaudy housings, fringed with little bells, that swept swirling and tinkling to the ground as they caracoled along. A number of masques wore stags' antlers and buffalo horns which rose above the heads of their fellows like the crests of condottieri and one or two wore carved and painted wooden heads with alarming and slanting eyes outlined in white paint. Gaping mouths were armed with long white tusks, and yellow manes of plaited straw and palm trash trailed down their backs. At the core of the masques danced two tall figures who seemed to hold some particular sway over their companions. One was a well-known sorceress and practitioner of *quimbois*, (the black magic of the islands), Maman Zélie: a hollow-cheeked crone in a white turban and a white dress, festooned in saltire with necklaces of coloured shells and beads. A short wooden pipe, smoking like a furnace, was irremovably clamped between her jaws, a white heart was painted on her forehead, and the rest of her face was patterned with bold rings and spirals of white. Beside her danced her invariable partner, the Devil King. He was dressed wholly in scarlet. A blood-red mask covered his face and his tall square cap, which was surmounted by a great flickering lantern, was adorned on each of its sides with a looking-glass and fringed all the way round with horses' tails.

As these newcomers danced in they sang a long incantation which was repeated half an octave lower at the end of each phrase, then once more at the initial pitch before the words altered. The musicians were masqued chalk-white, like zombies; their eyes were tight shut (the wearers peeped through slits in the eyebrows) and their buckram jaws hung cretinously open. The leaders wielded shackshacks: cylinders of bamboo filled with rattling seeds. They were followed by others who blew mournful and booming notes down *vaccins*: instruments made of two yards of bamboo several inches thick. Then came drummers with *Ka's*: rumkegs with skins stretched over either end. Others, bestriding long wooden tom-toms, moved forward, like ungainly insects, in little bounds. Two men dancing abreast stooped under a long beam on which three giants hammered deafeningly with clubs. (When these broke, they were speedily supplied with new ones by acolytes who carried sheaves of them in reserve.) Next came one who defined the tune on a shrill reed instrument like a primitive clarinet which somehow dominated the rhythmic din of his colleagues with a high-pitched, syncopated and unflagging scream. He was accompanied by two *banza* players strumming on rough stringed instruments made of half-calabashes and laths. Lastly a dozen zombies bore, aloft and horizontal, a giant tom-tom fashioned out of the hollow trunk of a tree. This was twelve feet long and a yard in girth and astride it, high above the tossing jungle of horns and antlers, higher even than the great central chandelier (whose pendant prisms, brushed by the perched drummer's crouching back, tinkled murmuring together in an impotent and inaudible *dix-huitième* protest at the pandemonium unloosed below), a frenzied rider was mounted. His bare palms hammered the drumhead at a lightning pace and each blow sent such an explosion of sound down the great wooden concavity between his legs that the very candles trembled in their hurricane glasses. In the space of a minute the elegant saloons, the fluted pillars, the white walls with their pale painted population of vanished Serindans – perruqued and fastidious grandees with the ribbon of the Holy Ghost across their sprigged satin waistcoats – their live descendants and all their guests, seemed to have melted away and their place to have been filled by the warriors, the witch-doctors and the blood-red splendour of the sacrificial groves of the Congo and Dahomey.

They fell into single file, each dancer holding the one in front of him by the hips, until the ballroom was girdled with a heaving chain of masques. The rhythm altered to the beat of the Mine dance – which originated, they say, on the Grain Coast – and everyone

stooped forward with their torsos swaying from side to
side and their bare feet, as they advanced, slapping the
polished floor in unison; leaping round at a signal crash
of the *bamboula* and continuing in the opposite direction
while, in the middle, the Sorceress and the Devil King,
stooping double, repeated the steps in a smaller compass.
At a break in the band's clangour, the dancers fished
gourds of rum and *tafia* from their disguises and took
quick pulls and even offered them to their neighbours
and to the guests that stood nearest. Many of them had
been drinking all through the last days of carnival and
were now in a state of amiable and harmless drunkenness. It was plain to see that the most advanced were the
half-dozen dominoes who rocked visibly on their feet
whenever the dancing stopped.

'Incidentally,' Berthe said, 'the champagne and rum
had been circulating continually since the ball began,
and with that, the noise, the dancing and the stifling
heat, many of the guests were in no better state –
especially some young men from the outlying plantations.'

The drums broke out once more in a violent tattoo,
and the women and the men arranged themselves in two
opposing lines. Hunching their shoulders behind craning
heads, they began to shuffle and shake and shudder in
the first steps of the *caleinda*. Setting forward at a
warning scream of the wind instrument, they advanced
two steps and retreated one, until, reaching their partners
opposite, they revolved round each other, jerking
and grunting, several times; retreating again to their

starting places, then forward and round each other back to back; then facing each other with their hips jerking in unison, and finally, almost on their knees, in frog-like postures, with their cheeks laid against those of their partners and their buttocks and shoulders jerking in quadruple time. Everything heaved and quaked, antlers interlocked with buffalo horns, and, against the hollow booming of the *vaccins* and the grinding percussion of the tree-trunk, the battery of tom-toms, goaded on by their screaming drummers, sounded as though it would break the instruments to smithereens under the pitiless and long-drawn-out hail of massed impacts.

The party from Government House, who had never seen such a sight, were bewildered. The Governor kept repeating that it was 'fort interessant, ma foi! Personne ne sait danser comme les nègres!' The Count resisted the temptation to tell him that the word *nègre*, as opposed to *noir*, was never used in the Islands except as an insult. But Madame Sciocca's hands were clasped in an ecstasy of metropolitan rapture. 'Mais ils sont impayables, ces gens là,' she cried to the Count at her side; then, as a more premeditated comment: 'quelle incroyable désinvolture!', she sighed.

Positions were soon taken up for a *bélé*,[1] a dance which was often accompanied by satirical words which were improvised afresh every season. With the first movements of the dance, the voices of the masques began singing:

1. *Bel air.*

Missié le Comte li bon béke,[1]
Et Maitw' Moustache ka wien savé,
Hié' soi' a six . . .

But, quelled in mid-line by frantic waves from the
Count, who rose precipitately from his chair, they got
no further. The tune had already provoked a simmer
of suppressed giggles and anxious looks among the
creoles, for the song, dealing with the conflict between
the Count and the Governor very much at the
Governor's expense, had been the rage of Plessis for the
last two months. Fortunately, nobody seemed to have
explained this to the Governor and his party, who,
naturally, could not understand the creole patois and
seemed ignorant of the Governor's universal nickname
of *Maître Moustache*. The tune changed, but not soon
enough to drown a loud, rather tipsy guffaw and a
shout of *Bravo!* from the door of the library, where one
of the most violent of the younger creole faction,
Gontran de Chambines, was uncertainly leaning with a
full glass of punch tilted in his hand at a precarious angle.

'Why did you stop the tune?' the Governor asked,
his forehead puckered in mystification. 'I've been
whistling it for days.' He did so once more, beating
time with his pince-nez.

'My dear Governor,' the Count whispered, 'it's
the *words* – les pawoles sont un peu shocking. You
know, the ladies, the bishop . . .' The Governor's brow
cleared and, with a gesture of knowing bachelor

1. White man.

collusion, he held out his glass for some more champagne.

The masques had started a *biguine*, the dance that more than any other typifies the fusion of African and French influences in the Antilles. At one moment it is European and formal and tinged by something of the touching and obsolete urbanity of a minuet: at the next, it slides into an essentially negro rhythm: African, spasmodic and Calypsonian. The one they had chosen was an old tune that had in some measure become the *leitmotif* of the French Antilles. The Count's orchestra joined with the carnival band. The masques fanned out and chose partners among the guests and, in a few moments, the room was a revolving constellation of heteroclite couples. M. de Serindan danced with Maman Zélie, Josephine with a masque dressed as a swordfish and draped in fishnet. Madame Sciocca, deploying a nice compound of diffidence and alacrity, accepted the arm of a young negro wearing an enormous pair of deer's horns: headgear which, the Captain murmured ominously in Berthe's ear, in view of his partner's growing cordiality with the Count, she might usefully borrow for future presentation elsewhere. ('Our national joke dies hard, you know,' Berthe inserted parenthetically.) The Governor was led through the complicated steps by the experienced hands of La Belle Doudou, the most resplendent and prosperous of the disguised *matadores*. The astonishing head-dresses, turning and nodding now in conjunction with the feathers and aigrettes of the creole ladies, while the spike-ended turbans and voluminous *douillettes* were escorted by the tall collars, the sashes and the starch of the creole squires, spun through verse after lilting verse. At the last one the *biguine* accelerated into a stampede and everyone joined in the words, which Berthe now softly sang once more in a deep and agreeable voice.

> *Toute moune tini*
> *Yon moune yo aimé,*
> *Toute moune tini,*
> *Yon moune yo chéwi.*

> *Toute moune tini*
> *Yon doudoux a yo*
> *Jusse moin tou sèle*
> *Pa tini ca, moin.*[1]

This breakneck maelstrom slowed down in cries and clapping and laughter and Gentilien shouted that supper was ready. The masques danced away to the lower terrace where a feast was prepared for them round an immense bowl of Martinique punch. The rest of the guests trailed through to the long lanterned terrace beyond the ballroom windows. A ninefold saraband of Muses dominated it from the balustrade with the swirl of their plaster draperies. 'It was about time,'

1. 'Everybody has somebody to love,' a rough translation would go, 'everybody has somebody to cherish, everybody has a sweetheart of their own, I alone can't have one, I alone.'

Berthe said. 'The air in the ballroom by this time had become stifling.'

★   ★   ★

Berthe broke off, filled the glasses and lit a new cigarette. The sparks of the flint lit up her face, summoning those hollows and salients for a split second out of the neutral moonlight and the shadows of the olive leaves. The moon, having cast loose long ago from the trees in front of us, was now travelling across the zenith of the sky. On the hair-thin and just describable line of the horizon beyond the silently spinning trunks, the Ægean hung in a shining and unruffled curtain.

'It is odd,' she said at last, 'how well I remember every detail of that night. It all happened half a century ago and I don't suppose I've talked about it to anyone for almost as long. But hardly a day has passed without my thinking about it and trying to piece it together. A ball is almost a short lifetime in itself. Everything that happened beforehand retreats, for the time being, into a kind of pre-natal oblivion and the world waiting for you when you wake up next day seems as vague and shadowy as the eternity that waits beyond the tomb. Like somebody's life, the ball goes on and on and the incidents stand out in retrospect like a life's milestones against a flux of time whose miniature years are measured out in dance tunes.' She laughed, thoughtfully. 'Anyway,' she went on, 'I suppose one might say that by supper-time, Cousin Agénor's Shrove

Tuesday Ball had just about reached middle age and could look forward to a jovial maturity, a leisurely senescence and, in the fullness of time, a happy end. Earlier anxieties had all vanished and in spite of one or two minor mishaps, everything was going swimmingly. The hatchet was buried and forgotten, the two rival parties were, at least on the surface, on the best of terms. Knowing most of the omens, I thought I could predict a worried month or two for Madame de Serindan; but poor Cousin Mathilde was used to this, and Cousin Agénor always returned to her in the end more attentive and solicitous than ever. I also felt that the Governor and La Belle Doudou would not remain strangers for long. It was a relief to see that there had been no spark revived between his son and Josephine. They seemed in fact to be studiously avoiding each other. But Josephine was plainly in a state of great suppressed excitement: listening distractedly, answering *mal à-propos* and laughing nervously: signs of which I was a fool not to have taken more notice. Every time we danced past each other I would find her eyes fixed on mine with a peculiar intentness in which fear and entreaty were uppermost. Towards the end of the *biguine* our eyes met again. Still gazing over the shoulder of her swordfish partner with the same overwrought and undecipherable expression, Josephine thrust her lips forward in the *moue* of a kiss. I blew a kiss back into the air and smiled. But no answering smile came back. Her eyelids fluttered confusedly and she lowered her head, so that all I could see, as the dance carried us away into different streams, was the mass of black hair and the three gardenias pinned there.

'I, too, was in a strange state of mind, and filled with a disquiet and a misgiving which I found impossible to unravel. All this was complicated by the presence of Sosthène.

'His time in France had done nothing to change his early feelings of infatuation. He had written continuously from Saint Cyr: long love letters that often enclosed pages of poetry, some of it very good indeed. And on his return—a tall and charming young man now, and, like all his family, something of a beauty – this feeling had turned into a determination that we should marry, or, as he declared in moments of emotion, that he should perish. His appearance, and in many ways, his wild and highly strung nature were so similar to Josephine's that I would often find myself gazing at him covertly and wishing that things had been planned for me on more ordinary lines. For, when his present feelings should finally die away, there were plenty of solutions for him elsewhere of a kind that seemed forever denied to me. As it was, I was too fond of him to be able to pack him off to search elsewhere; also, too familiar with his sister's impulsiveness to treat his own wild promises merely as threats. Our positions, in their different ways, were too similar and too hopeless (though I could not explain to him that all my feelings of love and devotion had irrevocably centred on another member of his family) for me not to feel bound to him by the ties of an invalid suffering from the same disease. We had danced together most of the evening and when after supper (where he had been acting as host to the Governor's staff) he led me mysteriously away to a little kiosk beyond the top terrace and renewed his entreaties and his terrible alternatives, it was easy to see that poor Sosthène had drunk far too much champagne. He fell on his knees and caught me round the waist. His speech was more exaggerated than ever and his hair was all over the place. I tried to brush it straight with my hands but he kept shaking it angrily loose. Assurances that one loves somebody like a brother (or a sister for that matter) are not the most calming remedies for someone who is in the extremes of the malady of love. He cried out that unless I said I would marry him he would shoot himself, drown himself in the sea or even, pointing upwards at the angrily flaming crater (burning, it seemed, every minute brighter), dive down the Salpetrière. I was really anxious about what might happen and, begging him to give me until tomorrow night to decide, to which he unwillingly consented, I determined not to leave his side all the next day.

'At this point Lucienne came running up the steps shouting for me. Sosthène jumped to his feet and rushed into the trees. Lucienne caught me by the hand. "Berthe," she cried, "we've been looking for you everywhere. It is time to change for the play. Everything is ready, and Josephine is first for once. Come along quick, or we shall be late."'

Gathering up their skirts, Berthe and Lucienne ran

indoors and up to their bedrooms. The Count, his face glowing with excitement, was waiting on the landing. He gave them a friendly pat on the shoulders as they passed, saying, 'vite, vite, mes enfants, your public is waiting', and then hastened downstairs to put the finishing touches to the scenery on the stage which had been rigged up at the end of the ballroom during supper.

The one-act play the Count had written specially for the occasion a couple of months before was a slight, witty and sentimental little sketch called *Amour en Castille*. The actors wore pseudo-Spanish costume of the time of Alfred de Musset. 'It was full of charm and fun,' Berthe said, 'and exactly right for a diverting interlude in the ball.' They had been rehearsing it hard during the last few weeks but there had been several changes in the cast. The grotesque part of an elderly and rather clownish grandee, necessitating a false obesity padded out with a pillow, the Count had written for himself; but when the invitation to Government House had been sent out, he had lost his nerve and begged the Captain to play it. The two principal figures, that of the grandee's niece, Doña Paz, a jealously guarded beauty, and her suitor Don Fernando, a young Castilian hidalgo, had been destined for Josephine and Berthe respectively and rehearsals had gone forward. But suddenly, one morning a week before, Josephine had begged Berthe for their two rôles to be changed round. She had seemed so set on it, that, slightly bewildered, both Berthe and the Count had consented. All the family, except for the

Countess and Sosthène, whose late arrival would have cut rehearsal time too short, were included. Anne-Jules had insisted on Pierrot's participation as a page and ally to his own rôle of rascally valet, and their exile to bed had been summarily rescinded. (As a matter of fact, neither of them had gone there in the first place. They had retired instead to the friendly obscurity of the kitchen to console themselves on secret feasting for the

loss of Sardanapalus.)

'Everything considered,' said Berthe, 'it all went off very well. As you can guess, I felt in no state for acting in a play, but luckily I have always been able to disguise my emotions. But Josephine was more excited and erratic than ever. She missed her cue several times, repeated the same stanza of a serenade twice and struck the last chord so violently that two of the guitar-strings broke. But by that time of the night the audience was in such good humour that it was an immense success. Josephine looked ravishing. Her boyish figure was dressed in a high-collared, tight-waisted black coat and a white stock. Tight black pantaloons were strapped under her boots and small silver spurs were screwed to her heels. Her hair was brushed back into a knot and she had drawn a curly moustache along her upper lip with kohl. Fernando and Paz had to take call after call – the Captain, sweating like a river under his upholstery, kept thrusting us forward – and Josephine and I, hand in hand, bowed and curtsied a score of times to an uproar of clapping and cheers. Cousin Agénor, answering massed shouts of 'Author!' was beside himself with pleasure. Madame Sciocca fanned herself in transports of voluble delight and the Governor kept declaring that it was better than anything he had seen in Paris, que c'était pharamineux! The actors' hands were caught by admirers from below and they were made to jump from the stage and take part in a schottische on the freshly powdered floor while the stage was cleared away.'

In the middle of this dance a deep and ominous rumble was heard above the notes of the orchestra. A bright flash like lightning drowned the many candle flames for a second with its brighter intensity and a rush of wind filled the curtains in their confining coils of hibiscus and blew them into the ballroom in wavering cylinders. The dancers stopped and looked through the long windows at the top of the Salpetrière where a sparkling fountain of fire had suddenly sprung to a great height in the air; a brilliant red gold needle, whose mounting summit bore all the gazing eyes upwards and then down again as it broadened and lost its shape and subsided. A wide stream of lava burnt its way down from the crater's rim to the waiting *chaudières*.

This diversion was greeted, as though it were a firework display, with claps and with shouts of 'vive la Salpetwière!' and 'à la bonne heure!' and when it had passed, the dance swept forward with a new vigour. It looked as if the volcano itself were conspiring with the Count to add lustre to his rout.

Berthe, meanwhile, had shed her combs and her shawls, kicked off her hooped black satin crinoline and put on her ball dress again. As she reached the ballroom, she felt an arm slid through hers. It was the Captain's.

'Berthe,' he exclaimed, 'you were a marvel. Come and have a glass of champagne this instant.' It was the first time she had seen him even slightly tipsy and, amused, she followed him into the library.

*   *   *

The noisy room beyond, usually the Count's study, had been turned for the evening into a smoking-room. It was one of the pleasantest and most lived-in rooms of the house and it was only out of bounds to the rest of the family when the Count was in the pangs of one of his sudden onslaughts of creative fever. The walls were covered with bookcases and the horns of strange animals. A stuffed Jacobean heron, with petunia-

coloured breast-feathers, a duck-billed platypus, two
toucans, a wombat, a quetzal and three birds of paradise,
one of them with tail feathers ascending in a wonderful lyre, were immured in glass. Over the chimneypiece,
an apt symbol of the Count's Confucian tendencies,
was a vast genealogical tree whose timbers glittered
with impalements and quarterings and augmentations.
The roots were inscribed with the name of Gaultier de
Serindan, Seigneur de la Charce, Bailli of Fontenay and
Vidame of Luçon in the reign of Phillipe IV le Bel. Its
ample and heavily-loaded boughs spread like those of an
immense and overgrown pear tree basking espalierwise
on an orchard wall; branch sprang from branch with the
advance of generations, diminishing at last to the smallest
and most recent twig, neatly labelled with the name of
Anne-Jules. (On the day of her arrival Berthe had been
conducted to this forest giant and the Count's long and
unerring fore-finger had alighted triumphantly on the
skeleton leaf where the scarcely legible name of her
own great grandmother was inscribed: Athenaïs de
Serindan, married in 1782 to the Chevalier Armand de
Rennes, who was killed in the fighting at Nouaille in
the Vendée on the same day as La Rochejaquelein.) The
rest of the room was a jungle of globes, astralabs,
telescopes, albums, ancient maps, sheet music and old
instruments of all kinds. The harpsichord, M. de Serindan
would affirm, had once belonged to Lulli, and round this
treasure were grouped a rebeck, a cromorne, a theorbo
and a tromba marina. There were vessels containing
snakes in spirits and a large case of great blue-green

butterflies from Cayenne. Usually some newly arrived acquisition from Paris occupied the centre of the room – a magic lantern, a kaleidoscope or, that particular year – for the Count was determined to own the first horseless carriage in the island – an elaborate working model of the de Dion-Bouton motor car that he had just ordered; and a game of puff-billiards. Many of these treasures had been put on one side before the ball to make room for the present occupants of the study. But its tutelary genius, an immense and splendid macaw from Nicaragua called Triboulet, still presided on his accustomed perch, silencing the hubbub from time to time with a screech and a succession of clicks, followed by the words, 'Montjoy– Saint Denis!' or, alternatively, the only words that the Count had mastered in English: *Have a dwink*!

The injunctions of this bird had not been falling on deaf ears. From where she sat Berthe could see the Jacobean squires leaning against the desk and spread at their ease across the chairs and sofas in their white suits and red sashes. Long cheroots were stuck between their teeth and there were rum-glasses in their hands. (A closet beyond was exclusively devoted to the changing of collars, whose rigidity melted into damp shapelessness with the heat and vigour of half a dozen dances. Ardent performers – six-collar-men – had sent on their servants in advance with a liberal supply of fresh collars and white cotton gloves.) Thick clouds of tobacco smoke, creeping out into the library and hanging in layers round the candelabra, streamed in horizontal drifts through the windows and into the dark. In the doorway Marcel Sciocca and another member of the Government House party were talking to a nephew of the Count's, who, in default of Sosthène, was looking after them. Sciocca was paying little attention to the conversation and every now and then he drew a watch from his pocket in a manner which spelled either boredom or preoccupation.

'That evening was the first time I had a chance of seeing him close to,' Berthe said. 'He had gone out of his way to be agreeable all the evening with a ghastly kind of shop-walker's gallantry. He was as vain as a peacock. But I don't think that it was entirely the exasperation and anger that I felt when I thought that we were, or had been, rivals, that deepened my feelings that he was a man capable of any despicable action. There was nothing beyond a vague field of rumour and unfavourable surmise to base this on. Certainly he was not to blame for what happened next, beyond a remark which was, in the circumstances, very unfortunate. The fact that he and Gontran de Chambines came anywhere near each other at all was mere bad luck.'

Gontran de Chambines de la Forest d'Ivry and his twin brother François, Berthe explained, were something of a problem to their family and to Jacobean society in general. They lived a wild life on their estate at Pointe d'Ivry, a steep cape at the north end of the Island where they drank, as Berthe put it, like holes, and spent their sober hours riding and shooting with their negroes and organising cock-fights and contests between snakes and mongooses. Extremely likeable and as gentle as lambs when sober, drunk they were the reverse. Their inflammable tempers and their recklessness made them prone to rash acts and their careers had been a long succession of scrapes. They were tall, strong, florid creatures with choleric, Norman-looking blue eyes. Gontran was only distinguishable from François by a stutter which, when both of them were in their cups, became slightly more pronounced than that of his twin. Both of them, most unfortunately in this instance, were advanced and violent partisans of what Government House described in their reports as 'the Creole Obscurantist Reaction'. Their two bass voices, now galloping forward, now held up at the hurdle of an awkward consonant, had dominated the noise from the Count's study for the past hour or two, growing steadily louder and more garbled as the laughter and tinkle of breaking punch glasses increased in frequency. When they appeared arm-in-arm in the library door, their already sodden aspect turned by the heat into that of complete ragamuffins, it was obvious that they could hardly stand. Damp sequins of tipsiness swam in their four blue eyes above two smiles of inane felicity. Gontran, losing his footing in the crowded threshold, swayed dangerously, knocking over a chair. Sciocca, wisely flattening himself against the wall to avoid the danger zone – ineffectually, as Gontran, lurching in the same direction, collided with Marcel Sciocca's shoulder before regaining his precarious balance – dislodged a small engraving from a constellation of miniatures beside the bookcase. It fell to the floor and the glass broke. Gontran managed to articulate an incoherent apology and prepared to resume his rambling progress, and Sciocca stooped and picked up the picture and the broken glass. Considering the persons involved it had been a dangerous moment. But Gontran had failed to recognise his neighbour and the spectators, who had watched in agony, breathed again. Sciocca, before putting the frame back on its hook, lifted some black silk that hung from the ring and glanced at the picture. His eyebrows went up. 'Tiens!' he said, holding the engraving at arms' length. He tilted his head to one side in a posture of facetious scrutiny and read out loud the legend printed underneath. '*L'exécution à Vincennes le vingt-et-un mars, mille huit cent quatre, de Son Altesse Royale le Prince Louis Antoine Henri de Bourbon-Condé, Duc d'Enghien*.' Looking up with the air of somebody about to append a witty footnote to a tedious text, he went on, 'Ce n'était vraiment pas la peine de l'abattre deux fois.' He raised the picture, 'C'est fouetter un chat mort, comme qui dirait.'

Berthe broke off at this point, lit a cigarette and meditatively allowed a thread of smoke to climb into the olive branches before continuing. 'The odd part of it,' she said in the end, 'is that I don't think Sciocca meant any harm. After all, the shooting of the Duc d'Enghien was ancient history. Certainly, in ordinary circles, nothing to make a song and dance about any longer. And I suppose Sciocca's remark was nothing more than a rather inept and pointless, but rather caddish, joke.

(In fact, Sciocca's complacent expression of mild banter and the scattering of titters his words evoked amongst some of the Metropolitans, rather proved this.) He may, with the best will in the world, have been trying to pass off Gontran's drunkenness and the silly collision as a joke, or he may have intended it as a sly dig (I think it is called) at the antiquated prejudices of the Jacobeans. Or, bearing in mind what happened later, he might have said it merely from nerves and distraction and the desire to chatter lightly and unconcernedly at all costs. But, whatever it was, the creoles were thunderstruck with horror; partly because Sciocca's words seemed a gratuitously wounding sneer, and in the circumstances, very impertinent, but mostly out of anxiety about their effect on Gontran de Chambines. Any goodwill Sciocca had acquired by virtue of his earlier amiability was squandered in a second. Nobody seemed to find anything to say, not even the Captain. I felt his finger and thumb tighten apprehensively on my elbow as Sciocca spoke. Gontran had stopped in his tracks. Still swaying, he supported himself with one hand on the doorpost. His eyes slowly focused themselves on Sciocca. Then, opening wide with a fixed and owlish stare we all knew only too well, his face appeared to swell and grow crimson with mounting rage. When he spoke after the tentative titters had died down, he had almost lost his voice. It came out halting and strangled.

'M-Monsieur,' he said with difficulty, 'v-voilà une p-p-p-plaisantewie que je ne g-goute que m-m-médiocwement.' His comment was unexpectedly mild and rather comically pompous. The uninitiated Sciocca, deceived by Gontran's glassy stare and scarcely audible voice, must have thought that he had been presented with a heaven-sent butt. His eyebrows went up still further in a pert facsimile of surprise. 'Ah?' he said, imitating not only Gontran's tone of voice but his creole accent. and his stammer, 'and w-why are y-you only m-mediocrely am-m-mused?'

Gontran's face went black with rage. His arm shot out and, seizing Sciocca by the front of his shirt and crumpling it fiercely with an enormous hand, he jerked Sciocca towards him and croaked 'P-p-parceque v-vous êtes une s-sale b-b-bête.' Sciocca seized Gontran's wrist and tried to shake him off, then struck him on the chest. He had gone as white as paper and both men were trembling all over with fury. Gontran lurched, recovered his balance, and, still gripping Sciocca by his shirt, which was beginning to tear, caught him a violent blow on the side of one cheek and then one on the other with the back of his hand, and threw him free against the wall. It was a horrible scene. Sciocca was the first to recover. Red finger-marks showed across his face.

'I'll have satisfaction for this,' he said, 'tomorrow when he is sober.'

'G-good,' Gontran answered in gulps. 'Ask him to tell a f-fwiend, if he's got one, to g-get in t-touch with my b-bwother.'

Sciocca looked questioningly at the man standing beside him, who nodded assent.

'Monsieur Lambert, my father's ADC will represent

me,' Sciocca said. Then, looking at his watch, he bowed
in a stagily ironical manner, exposed a couple of golden
grinders in a smile, and turned towards the french window. His second made as though to follow him, but
Sciocca held up his hand with a murmur of 'later on!'
Then saying 'à demain' in a loud, clear voice, he walked
out alone into the dark.

The whole incident took less than a minute, and,
somehow, passed miraculously unnoticed by the dancers
revolving continuously past the library door. Everyone
was slightly nonplussed, and also impressed by Sciocca's
composure, which, in a measure, took the wind out of
their indignation while it increased their dislike. Gontran, of course, had behaved outrageously, as usual. But,
unfairly, and in spite of Gontran having shown himself to be a drunken boor, the sympathy was all on
his side. Yet the incident had occurred, as it were,
in creole territory and the opposition were guests and
a minority. Everyone felt thoroughly uncomfortable.
The Captain was the first to recover. Gontran, re-
lapsing into his previous state with photographic
abruptness, was conducted back into the study and
persuaded 'to rest' on a sofa, where he was soon
peacefully snoring. Summoning all the witnesses, perhaps a dozen, to the window, the Captain easily persuaded them to tell nobody about the incident, and least
of all the Count or the Governor, until every other
means of preventing an encounter had been attempted in
vain. A meeting between Chambines and Sciocca
threatened not only the usual dangers incident to such

affairs, but the definitive and total breakdown of the reconciliation, which, until the recent accident, had been going so rosily. Gontran, whose last words before falling asleep had been a bloodthirsty boast about 'making a hole in that animal's hide', was better left undisturbed for the moment.

The Captain took Berthe aside and begged her to find Sosthène (of whom Gontran was very fond) who was clearly the person, reinforced by Berthe, to reason with him when he came round. Sciocca had disappeared, so the Captain got to work on his second, Monsieur Lambert, who was in complete agreement about the calamitous possibilities ahead. Unfortunately, Gontran's brother and second, leaning out of the window at the far end of the library in a state close to collapse, was in no fitter plight to discuss matters than his principal. Gontran was known to be equally formidable with rapier and sabre and pistol; but, violent and *spadassin* when drunk, he was also, especially waking up after a night like this, both penitent and tractable. Monsieur Lambert, an intelligent and rather agreeable man, had no light to shed on Sciocca's lethal proficiency or his accessibility to reason, except the admission, accompanied by a dubious shake of the head, that he was 'un homme très rancunier . . .'

Their deliberations were interrupted by the sepulchral voice of François de Chambines from the window: 'L-look,' he said, 'it's s-snowing.' The observation was so unexpected and irrelevant that everybody burst out laughing. And snow was indeed falling. It was that light descent of feather-soft ash that often followed any unusual activity of the Salpetrière. It glittered in daylight like hoarfrost, and the Jacobean negroes used to call it 'saltpetre-snow'. They watched the silent, fluttering, windless descent across the lamplit window and, putting their arms outside, allowed the warm strange flakes, the only snowfall ever seen in the Antilles, to settle on their hands. Berthe found the Captain standing beside her.

'Berthe,' he whispered, 'do please go and find Sosthène.'

*   *   *

Sosthène, however, was nowhere. After a search all over the house, the gardens and the bedrooms, Berthe was on her way back to the library when her eye was caught by a line of light under a door next to the oratory, whose red sanctuary lamp was usually the only thing visible there, at the end of a long passage. (Beyond this door lay a billiard room, adorned, for some reason, with English sporting prints and an enlarged daguerreotype of Leo XIII.) It was an odd place for anybody to be, and thinking Sosthène might have retreated there, Berthe ran along the passage and opened the door. A faint star of light burned at the end of the shadowy room. A young man in black, not clearly discernible by the candlestick placed on the green baize, was standing by the end of the table with some papers in his hand which he quickly thrust inside his coat. Berthe stopped on the threshold in confusion and was about to leave with an apology when he called her name and, picking up the candle, ran towards her. It was Josephine, still dressed in the costume she had worn for the play.

'Josephine, darling,' Berthe exclaimed, 'what are you doing up here all alone? Do hurry up and change. Everybody's asking for you. Have you seen Sosthène?'

Josephine shook her head. Taking the candle from her, Berthe saw that she had been crying. The track of a tear had run through one side of the moustache that was still pencilled along her upper lip. Berthe touched it with her forefinger and saw that it was wet.

'I – I didn't want to go back to the ball . . .' Josephine began. Breaking off, she threw her arms round Berthe's neck and put her head on her shoulder in a sudden up-rush of weeping. Her hair came undone and fell down her back and her body was shaken by a deep and violent fit of tears. All Berthe could think of was saying 'there, there, my angel', folding her in her arms and stroking and comforting her as best she could.

Gradually this first wild intensity died down and sub-sided into a succession of wrenching and destructive sobs. At last Berthe tipped Josephine's head back, swept the damp hair away from her forehead and dried the tears away with her handkerchief. Josephine grew calmer and Berthe ventured to ask her what was the matter.

Josephine heaved a long sigh. 'It's nothing,' she kept repeating. 'I'm such an idiot and please, please forgive me, my own darling Berthe.' Berthe even managed with coaxing to conjure up the ghost of a rainy smile.

'I can't tell you how moving, how terribly touching

she looked,' Berthe said. 'That damp cheeked little hidalgo with her wide violet eyes and that smudged moustache and her hair falling in a long black tangle over one shoulder! But she would not tell me what it was all about, and promised to let me know next day. Almost recovered now, except, occasionally, for a dry and shuddering sob, she kept gazing at me with that queer light-headed fixity. So I pointed to the billiards-room clock and said: 'Look! It's a quarter to three. Run upstairs and wash in cold water, darling, and change and come down again.' She stiffened and made an effort to put on a brave face. 'Shall I come and help you?' She shook her head. 'No,' she said forlornly, 'I'll join you.' I picked the candle up and we walked along the passage with our arms around each other's waists. When we reached the foot of the stairs leading to the bedrooms, Josephine caught me by the shoulders and said, 'Dearest darling, darling Berthe. Will you promise to love me always?' I said of course I would. 'Always, always?' she repeated, putting her forehead against mine and gazing with such close fixity that her bright eyes under their single sweep of brow converged into one, like that of a cyclops. 'Always, *always*?' Then seizing me with a stronger grip than anything of which I had thought her capable, she gave me a long fierce hug. She broke away and caught hold of my hand and kissed it and then ran upstairs to her bedroom without looking round. I watched her running figure till all that was left were the little spurs twinkling on her heels in the candle light. Then they vanished in the darkness of the upper regions and I went slowly downstairs, wondering why she was so unhappy. I had forgotten all about the duel and Sciocca and Sosthène. . . .'

On the landing halfway down a tall fan-topped window, built during the interregnum when Saint-Jacques was an English colony, looked out over the tree-tops. It was hotter than ever and the sinister volcanic snow was still silently falling. The trees in shadow were as dark as ink. Every few seconds, a flicker from the Salpetrière, which was invisible at the other side of the house, cast a rufous glow over the tree-tops, all covered now with flakes of ash. The sound of singing, high carnival howls and the throb of drums rose from the town, and the great headdresses – the helms, now, under the white downfall, of Teuton Burgraves in the Lithuanian mists – were slanting and turning along the torchlit lanes. Beyond the lighthouse's turning beam, the red port light of an anchored sailing ship hung high in the darkness.

*   *   *

The buoyant rhythm of a waltz and the rumour of talk and laughter drowned the tom-toms of Plessis as Berthe came downstairs to the lights of the ballroom. She found the Count standing in the hall, his hair ruffled and his eyebrows twisted up in obvious distress.

'Really, Berthe,' he said, leading her into an antechamber, 'of all the things to happen, just when everything was going so well!'

Berthe asked what was the matter but he appeared not to have heard her.

'The best ball we've ever had,' he went on, 'and now this comes along and ruins everything.' He lowered his tall body despondently onto a sofa and, leaning an elbow on his knee, rested his bearded chin on his fist in an attitude of bewildered pensiveness. Somebody must have told him about the duel, Berthe thought. But it soon turned out to be something else.

'I thought there was something queer about those black dominoes from the start,' he went on. Completely at sea, Berthe could stand it no longer. She sat down beside him on the sofa. 'What about the black dominoes, Cousin Agénor?'

'You haven't heard? Thank God for that! Well, you noticed those black dominoes who came in with the carnival masques – the drunkest of the lot? Well, when the time came to unmask at half past two, I went down to their terrace with Gentilien to have a drink with the whole party. They did the usual *caleinda* and then off came the masks. Everything was very lively and gay. But the dominoes had all collected to one side and were about to slip away into the trees. The others saw them, and everyone shouted that the masks must all come off. A crowd of boys ran and pulled them back to the fireside. Everyone was laughing and Maman Zélie took charge and said they must each drink a full glass of rum as a forfeit. But they still refused to unmask and tried to run off again, so the others caught hold of them and the *Roi-Diable* ceremoniously threw back the first one's domino and lifted off his mask. And,' the Count lowered his voice, 'what do you think?' His voice fell still lower. 'It was a leper. And when the other five were unmasked, they all turned out to be lepers as well. There was a terrified silence at first. Then – you can imagine the up-roar . . . I tried to calm everybody down and sent Gentilien back to the house for Dr Vamel. The lepers were in such a condition they could hardly articulate. They had been loose in the town for the past five days, drinking hard all the time and never daring to join in the meals in case they were discovered. As you can guess, they were all as drunk as Poles, and it was very hard to make out how they got here. It seems that they came from the Desirade[1]. One of them had been there seven-teen years. Some time last week they stole a boat and headed for Marie Galante, meaning to hide there in the dominoes (which they had prepared beforehand) for the first few days of carnival. When the search for them in the Desirade and in Guadeloupe had died down, they planned to slip across and stow away on the Brest packet from Pointe-à-Pitre,[2] and make their way to France. A myth has apparently grown up in the Desirade that a new cure for the disease has been discovered in France which the local authorities know nothing about or are wilfully withholding. . . . At all events, off they set, steered much too far south, missed Marie Galante

1. La Desirade – the Deseada of the first Spanish Conquistadores – is the rocky coffin-shaped island some miles to the east of Guadeloupe and due north of Saint-Jacques. It is the principal leper colony of the French West Indies.
2. The port of Guadeloupe.

and finally landed here at Cap d'Ivry. They made their way to Plessis under cover of night, living on dasheen and yam and breadfruit they had uprooted from the plantations and lying up in the forest till it was dark, arriving here five days ago, when they were able to put on their dominoes and come out of hiding. . . .

'Dr Vamel was marvellous. He promised to see that they were properly looked after and I will do what I can for them as well. But, between ourselves, there is no hope. The cure is a complete legend,' the Count sighed. 'The masques behaved very well indeed. Dr Vamel told them, and I backed him up, that leprosy isn't usually contagious in the ordinary sense – not that you can ever be sure. You can touch people a hundred times without catching it. It is prolonged and intimate contacts that are the most dangerous, if you follow me; and that's half the trouble in this case. You know how drunk everybody gets and what goes on in carnival time. . . . The doctor said he would do what he could, with strong disinfectant, for anyone who felt himself or herself to be specially in danger. In the end, he left for his clinic with a very sad little procession of *Gwan-wobes*. . . . What a business! We all either danced with them or with people who *had*; so we are all potential lepers. Poor little Berthe! Toi et moi aussi, et la pauvre Mathilde et les enfants et le Capitaine et Gentilien et tous les invités et tous les noirs! But there's nothing to be done about it, absolutely nothing. The great thing is not to mention it to anybody, especially not to the *Metwopolitains*.'

'What has happened to them now?' Berthe asked.

'To the lepers? Gentilien and I locked them in the old coach house with a sucking pig and a demijohn of rum, poor fellows. We'll have to put our thinking caps on tomorrow. . . . Luckily,' he went on, waving to the ball-room, which seemed more densely and hilariously populated than ever, 'nobody seems to have heard yet and the best thing we can do is to forget all about it for the present.'

The Count promptly put his own precept into prac-tice. 'I really think it's the best ball we've ever had!' he said. 'Except for what we were just talking about. Everything has gone right from the start. I was afraid for a moment we might have trouble with Gontran and his brother. You know what they are. But, no – every-thing is going capitally.' He paused a moment, and then said, rather cautiously, 'You know, Madame Sciocca is a most delightful woman. Don't you think so?'

'Well . . .' Berthe began.

The Count raised his hand. 'I know! You haven't had time to get to know her yet! But she's a charming creature and so intelligent and amusing and very well read too! I'm sure you'll like her. And we were all totally wrong about the Governor too – he's quite a nice old stick, apart from his infernal politics; though, I'm bound to admit, rather a bore. . . . Of course nobody knows where the money comes from. But, I must say, I don't think I could ever get to like that ghastly son of his. He gives me goose flesh. I don't wonder his wife stayed behind in Paris.'

'His wife?'

'Yes, quite a nice little thing, she sounds. But I'd be ready to bet a thousand louis that he's a *vilain monsieur*. What do you make of him?'

'I think he's terrible.'

'Do you? Do you really?' He spoke as though Berthe's answer revealed a new aspect of Marcel Sciocca that had not previously been manifest. 'I am sure you're right.' The subject dropped and the Count hummed the tune of *Quand l'amour revient* which the band was playing, for a few seconds. 'Everybody is enjoying themselves, that's the great thing. Except,' his brow clouded again, 'poor Josephine. I don't know what's the matter with that child. I went up to get some more cigars about an hour ago and there she was, mooning about by herself in the billiard room passage. She leapt at my neck and embraced me as if her last hour had come. Do you know what's the matter?'

'No, I don't, Cousin Agénor.'

'Well, whatever it is, I hope she'll get over it soon. Then there's Sosthène. Wandering about ever since he got back like a mute at a funeral! Why, at his age, on a night like this, I'd have been through a dozen collars by now! Berthe, you're so clever and sensible, I wish you'd get them out of it.' The Count took one of her hands and held it for a moment between both of his. 'You know how happy Mathilde and I would be if you and Sosthène . . . Well, there's plenty of time to talk about *that*.'

He put her hand gently back on her lap and taking two water-ices from a tray held by Gentilien, he gave one of them to Berthe.

'Do try this,' he said, 'it's a new sort I am experimenting with – it's made out of mangoes and flavoured with kirsch. And just imagine, in three weeks time the motor car will be here! Think of all the picnics we'll have . . .' The Count's face, radiant once more, seemed to reflect the shining prospects ahead. It was suddenly distorted with a rictus of anguish. '*A-yi*!' he exclaimed. 'What a mess they are making of that tune! And we practised it scores of times. I must go and lend a hand.'

He leapt agilely to his feet and, catching sight of his reflection in a long *art nouveau* looking-glass surrounded by a plaster relief of lotus leaves and poppies, he said, 'I'm a complete scarecrow.' He flattened his disordered hair, straightened his Maltese cross, smoothed his moustache, and combed his strong forked beard out from the parting with his finger-tips.

'Really, this snow,' he murmured, dusting some flakes from his shoulders, 'we might be at Chamonix.' Then his mind jumped back to the motor car. 'And we could drive up the Salpetrière to the sulphur springs and bathe! Perhaps I ought to have ordered two motors. . . . After all, there's got to be room for the servants and the tent and the food. . . . Berthe, do go and tell Sosthène and Josephine about it. Nobody knows yet. Also,' he said with a mysterious smile, 'there are some more surprises ahead that I'd hate them to miss. It might cheer them up. Tell them everyone's asking for them. We'll have the greatest possible fun this spring,' he leant forward and whispered, 'if we are not all lepers by then!'

He turned at the doorway and with a serio-comic

expression shaped the last phrase silently once more:
'Pou'vu que nous ne soyions pas tous des Lépweux . . .'
and placed a finger across his lips conspiratorially. A
few moments later he was through the door and on
the orchestra platform with one of the negroes' violins
under his chin, alternately fiddling and beating the
measure with his bow, and reviving by word and
example the strayed rhythm of the *Washington Post*.

*   *   *

Gentilien was still standing behind the sofa. Once again
Berthe was struck by the resemblance between the two
men that centred on that thick single bar of joined eye-
brow. He had made signals that he had something
important and private to tell her as he handed the ices
and Berthe had done her best to hasten Monsieur de
Serindan back to the ballroom. Gentilien was agitated.
'Mademoiselle Berthe,' he began, holding out an envelope, 'Numa Pompilius has just discovered this.' Berthe
took the letter. It was a thick envelope, addressed to
her, with a big blue *J* entwined with embossed forget-
me-nots on the back. 'He discovered it in the wire
letter box behind the front door which was hooked
back, so nobody would have seen it until tomorrow,
if Numa had not gone there for a broom to sweep
some ashes away. Mademoiselle Josephine has been
so strange lately – Fanette is very anxious and I am
frightened something might happen to her . . .' Berthe,
meanwhile, after struggling to tear the envelope with
her finger, ripped it open with the handle of the ice

spoon. It contained several smaller envelopes addressed to the Count and the Countess and the other children and a sheet of paper with a message that ran as follows: *My Dearest Darling Berthe. When you read this tomorrow, my darling, I will be on my way to Paris and I am marrying him the second we get there. Please do not be cross or hate me but love me always and come and see me. I'll write at once and please, please explain everything to Papa and Maman. I can't help it darling, it's my fate, and you will love him as much as I do when you all know him. I kiss you tenderly again and again my darling only Berthe. Your Josephine.*

There were swollen smudges in places where tears had fallen on the ink, and two lines of crosses. Then in a different-coloured ink: *I have just said goodbye to you darling at the bottom of the stairs. You are so kind to me. I wish I were dead and I kiss you again and love you always. J.* × × × × ×

Berthe felt her heart beating fast. Looking at the clock she saw that it was twenty past three. She pushed the letter into the front of her dress and, seizing the butler's

arm, said, 'Quick, Gentilien! There may still be time.'
They ran along the passage and up the back stairs. A
couple were sitting on the top step with their hands
lying open on their knees and their eyes shut in a long
and motionless kiss. The two heads fell apart as Gentilien
and Berthe stepped between them and Berthe saw that
the girl was Lucienne, looking up at her with her lids
half open as though waking out of sleep. When she saw
who it was she jumped up with a cry of, 'oh!' but by
that time Berthe and Gentilien were halfway up the next
flight. Josephine's room was empty. Her white ball dress
was thrown across a chair. The white satin shoes lay beside it and the carpet was scattered with a constellation
of gardenias. The sheets and the pillows under the
drawn mosquito net were rumpled to look as though
Josephine were asleep inside. But the dressing table had
been pulled away from the window and, running over
to it, Berthe saw a narrow footmark of French chalk
from the ballroom floor printed on the polished sill.
Outside, the branches of an immense *ceiba tree* almost
touched the wall.

'It was a way down,' Berthe said, 'that we had often
used together – more for the excitement of it than from
any real need for secrecy. It was only a hop from the
window on to the nearest branch, then you climbed
from one branch to another almost as easily as walking
downstairs and slid down the ropes of a swing on to the
grass. But there was nobody about below, nothing but
the lawn and then the steep forest and not a movement
anywhere except the falling flakes. Where could she

have gone? All at once I remembered Marcel Sciocca's repeated glances at the time, his sudden departure after the challenge, the alacrity of Josephine's flight upstairs at the approach of three o'clock. . . . Where would they hide, I wondered, in so small an island? There wasn't a boat for over a week. . . . Then the whole thing suddenly became clear. That light out in the bay! I ran across the landing and looked out of the front window. It was still there. There was no time to lose. "If only Monsieur Sosthène were in!" I said out loud.

"'Monsieur Sosthène? But I saw him come in about ten minutes ago. Perhaps he is in his room." Gentilien picked up the petrol lamp and we went down the passage. No light showed under the door and there was no answer to Gentilien's knocking and his cries of "Monsieur Sosthène!" Remembering Sosthène's threats, in a sudden access of alarm I told him to go in. The door was unlocked and I followed him inside. Sosthène was lying with his face to the wall. I opened the mosquito net and put my hand on his shoulder. Without moving he said: "Leave me alone, Gentilien, can't you?" When he heard my voice he turned over in surprise and sat up. He was covered with ash, his uniform was torn and soaking with dew and one leg was covered up to the knee with marsh slime. He must have been wandering about in the forest ever since he had run away from me at the kiosk in the garden. He was the very picture of misery. Before he could say anything I sat down beside him and told him in a few seconds what was happening. He jumped to the floor before I could finish and, shouting for Gentilien to follow, took my hand and ran downstairs. They could not have left the house more than half an hour ago and if we made haste there was a good chance of overtaking them. Obviously, he said, the ship was waiting out there to pick them up. What would an island boat be doing out to sea on Shrove Tuesday? He and Gentilien decided that the main street through Plessis running down to the Place Hercule and the Mouillage (as the harbour was called) would be blocked with merrymakers, for most of the population of the island streamed to the capital for the last days of the carnival. So we determined to follow the path through the forest. If we took one of the waiting carriages, we would only be able to move through the town at a crawling pace.

'I stopped and looked down from the landing on the way, in the wild hope that perhaps Sciocca – or even Josephine – might suddenly appear in the ballroom below, but, of course, neither of them was there. I can only have stayed a few seconds but the details remain in my mind as indelibly as a photograph. The scene had never been more animated. Beyond the three great intervening chandeliers that hung below like so many glittering cocoons of revolving insects, lay the whole brilliant apparatus of the ball. There seemed no room to move and yet round and round swung the couples in a great tangle of interweaving eddies, and waves of laughter and music and heat rose from the dancers almost visibly. Cousin Agénor was dancing with

Madame Sciocca and the Governor – for many of the masques had returned from the garden – with La Belle Doudou. Lucienne was there with Prosper des Chaumes, her cavalier of the back stairs, and Solange with her cousin Blaise de la Popelinière. Gontran and François, magically resurrected, were singing the ballad about Charette, the leader in the Vendée rebellion – a great song in the part of France I came from – their arms interlocked with several birds of the same feather who had reached a pitch almost equal to their own. Anne-Jules, in spite of the noise, had fallen asleep in a chair. The Captain, a little surprisingly, was dancing spiritedly in the middle of the room with the young negro dressed as a swordfish who had partnered Josephine in the *biguine*. Cousin Mathilde, looking tired, was sitting in a *causeuse* by the great window, talking to the bishop. Glancing up towards my vantage point she caught sight of me and, with a tired smile, waved her fan in a friendly and charming greeting across the rotating heads.

'No stranger, looking down as I was, could have suspected that the house was at that very moment beset by the prospect of a duel, by the start of a lasting feud that would split the island irreconcilably, by the threat of the suicide of the son and heir, by the elopement and possibly the bigamous marriage of the eldest daughter and by the universal menace of leprosy. I felt a kind of melancholy omniscience as I gazed down, a dismal certainty that I was the only person aware of all the hazards and sorrows ahead, and the memory of those few moments is still so startlingly clear in all its details that it might have been the result of a long scrutiny, consciously pursued with the purpose of printing on my memory the family and the house and the friends and the life that had become my own. It was as though I knew that I would never see any of it again.

'I joined Sosthène and Gentilien at the bottom of the back stairs. They had both taken cutlasses for the undergrowth and as we passed the yard, which was now as white with flakes as Spitzbergen, the carriages were beginning to assemble once more for the eventual departure of the guests. Gentilien slid two coach lamps from their brackets on a waiting Victoria and handed one of them to Sosthène.

*   *   *

'The sound of raucous and disjointed singing came from the barred windows of the old coach house where the lepers were locked up.

'It was almost hotter out than indoors and as we ran over the lawns to the two stone nymphs where the little-used path through the forest began, the flakes were falling so thick that it was hard to see. But once under the branches, the air cleared and not a flake penetrated the thick roof of leaves. The path led away westwards from Plessis, round the shoulder of a hill and down a ravine. The music of the ball and of the drums of Plessis soon fell silent, but the stillness of the forest was broken by the startled noises of the birds stirring overhead – an alarmed and unusual chorus of whistling and chattering. The rhythmic croaking of thousands of frogs sounded through the trees, but all the forest noises were dominated by the unbroken, high-pitched and metallic cry of the Jacobean cricket which, with the shrill urgency of a stop-watch, seemed to say *Make haste*!

'The narrow track went steeply down, turning and turning on itself like a winding staircase so that the dancing coach lamps revolved through the leaves and the ferns ahead of me in erratic descending circles. Holding the lamps high overhead, Sosthène and Gentilien only halted a moment in their course – borne up, it appeared, by the pale winding currents of the forest mist that reached as high as their armpits – to slash with their cutlasses through a hindering loop of convolvulus or wild vine. I soon threw my shoes away, and, catching up my enormous skirt, pursued them over the damp humus of the path in stockinged feet. Outside the radius of the two lamps all was black except for the polygonal dartings of millions of fireflies. A sudden flare from the crater of the Salpetrière would sometimes turn the sky beyond the tree-tops deep red, and, for a few flickering moments, light the enormous liana-tangled architecture of the forest with a faint and infernal glare. Tripping at a turn in the path over what I thought was a stone, I fell full length. When they stopped to help me up, my stumbling block proved to be an armadillo which had rolled itself into a tight ball. The lamplight also revealed a whole army of small fauna retreating downhill – frogs and lizards, an agouti or two, and, here and there, a

snake; a sluggish gibnut was lumbering along in the
middle of a flurried clouder of wild cats. Overhead,
thick flights of pigeons and blue parrots, and even
siffleurs montagnes, were on the move in flight from the
growing heat in the *chaudières* higher up the mountain's
flank. Gentilien's eyes in the lamplight were two
emblems of alarm. He crossed himself and muttered,
"Je n'aime pas ça!'"

Berthe's face was in shadow and we were both
looking out to sea, but a change in the volume of her
voice told me that she had turned her head in my
direction, when she said, 'To show you how quickly the
events of the last few minutes had happened, when I
picked myself up I found that I was still holding in my
hand the silver spoon that I had used for opening Josephine's letter.' Her voice resumed its normal pitch.
'Then our breakneck descent continued. To the right
of the path the forest sloped to a narrow creek
that was thickly choked by mangroves and then,
curling round the foot of the hill, it led to a small
lagoon separated by a tongue of land from the Mouillage. The Serindan boathouse, the starting point for so
many happy bathing parties in the past, was built out
here on piles among the arching mangrove trunks.
They broke open the lock with their cutlasses. We all
climbed into the little skiff, the two men put out their
lamps and shoved out into the sea with their oars.

'In the darkness of the bay, the ship's light was still
burning. It shed a still red line of light across the windless water. It was no longer snowing, and apart from

the splash of the oar-blades and the creaking of the row-locks, all was silent. As we drew level with the cape that separated the little lagoon from Plessis and the Mouillage, the glow of carnival lamps began to reappear through the palm tree stems along the headland and the sounds of rejoicing once more sounded in our ears. We passed the rock where a conclave of pelicans was always huddled, and our passing scattered them unwieldily into the dark.'

Berthe's narrative was punctuated every few minutes or so by the necessity of lighting a new cigarette to replace the one which had just come to an end: an unbroken life-line of tobacco in which these knots measured off her story in regular but arbitrary periods. Before taking up the thread of her story after the next of these caesurae, she digressed for a while in a more speculative tone of voice. 'I don't think any of us had a clear idea of what we would say and do if we succeeded in overtaking the runaways. Everything had happened so quickly and we had set off at such speed that there had been no time for a definite plan. I felt sure, however, that it would not have been difficult to persuade Josephine of the madness of continuing her flight. Her letter, I thought, showed the state of turmoil in her mind. We could always tax Sciocca with the fact that he was running away from a duel, and, still more pertinently, that he already had a wife in France – a fact which, still judging by Josephine's letter, he had not disclosed to her. As a last resort, I suppose there remained force, though this might not be easy on board a ship which had plainly been specially chartered, and presumably from another island, by Sciocca for the elopement. Perhaps we could have appealed to the crew, or, in the last event, have refused to disembark once we got on board. The revelation that Sciocca was already married had come as no surprise. It was, in fact, if properly handled, a distinct advantage on our side, as, should we catch them up, the confrontation of Sciocca with the fact might – though I didn't know how many shocks Josephine's infatuation could survive – have been the one thing that would decide Josephine to return with us to Plessis. If we should fail to overtake them, Sciocca's marriage would still, in the long run, be an advantage, as any form of marriage with Josephine would be invalid – a thing that would reinforce the fact that she was still a minor. Also, with the delays involved in a divorce, it would give Josephine a longer breathing space before there was any question of her contracting a civil marriage. But, as I said, I felt convinced that none of all this would be necessary and that, the moment we appeared, Josephine would fly into our arms.

'The more I thought of it, the more certain I became that Sciocca had virtually cast a spell over Josephine. It was obvious that the elopement had been planned some time ago, and the reason for Josephine's insistence on the change of parts in the play became apparent all at once. Knowing her, I felt sure that she had not broken her promise to me that she would not see Sciocca. But they had obviously been in contact by letter – Gentilien thought that the new servant, Hiram Abif, had been the go-between – in order to arrange the preparations for flight; and, indeed, Sciocca could not have chosen a night more likely to succeed. I suddenly understood something of her curious state the last few weeks. The poor darling wretch had been wandering about with her enormous and guilty secret in a sort of trance, a condition from which she only emerged to break into semi-hysterical tears, or behaviour that was very close to real folly. I am afraid I have made her appear a terrible cry-baby. Very often she had seemed to be on the point of telling me something, and each time something had stopped her, and when we were in the same room, whenever I looked up, I had found her eyes gazing at me with a sort of pathetic questioning fixity. And now, here she was, in the thick of a tenth-rate melodrama with unlimited possibilities of unhappiness and squalor – a mess that might well mean the destruction of her whole life just as it was about to begin. Apart from any other defects that Sciocca may have possessed, the fact that he could consciously involve so young and beautiful and vulnerable a creature in such a programme of inevitable sordidness, was an apt measure of his vanity and his lack of sensibility. I will spare you the feelings of desperate misery that I felt, and of powerless anger at the waste and destruction ahead, should the expedition we were embarked on come to nothing.'

Such were the thoughts that revolved in the mind of Berthe as she sat at the tiller of the skiff. They were probably not very different in the main from the cogitations at work in the two heads, now bent in silence over the oars, of Sosthène and Gentilien. The old fort on the headland, and then the revolving glow of the lighthouse at the end of the mole, were soon behind them; and as they advanced at a slant across the bay towards the far-away point where the ship's light still beckoned them, the Mouillage with its shoal of canoes and fishing boats and the long lantern-hung tangle of the masts of the sloops and the Leeward Island schooners, lengthened with each stroke of the oars. The long waterfront expanded. The distances widened between the statues posturing along the quay and spaced out the white balloons of the gasoliers. The little skiff reached the causeway, which was marked by two buoys at the ends of the coral reefs enclosing the harbour's entrance, exactly opposite the centre of the town; and the procession of the glowing water-front pillars, linked by the spans of arches diminishing along an oblique vista in the lessening trajectories of a bouncing ball, slowly readjusted itself into symmetry. Above this arcade the steep and shining amphitheatre of Plessis climbed in an acute-angled triangle of houses that was veined and split up by the streets – all of them choked, as though brilliant insects thronged them, by the heaving and torch-bearing revellers. Every roof and ledge and lintel was deep in the saltpetre-snow, and, in the lamplight, everything flashed white and gold. Plessis had been turned by magic into a chryselephantine town. Antlers and horns and bats' wings and feathered head-dresses leapt and turned in the ascending highways, showing black for a moment in mid-air and then subsiding into the rocking and sparkling anonymity of the crowd. Scores of drums rattled and the air trembled with the percussion of bamboo, while the long wooden horns moaned as though the hosts of Joshua were loosening the parapets of Jericho. The metamorphosis of night and snow and the many flames of carnival had turned the small Antillean town into a high and fabulous city poetically sailing into the darkness to outleap the ghosts of Troy and Ecbatana and balance on its uttermost pinnacle the overflowing and lamplit trees, the hanging gardens and the statued terraces of the Count de Serindan. The lilt of strings floated down through the hot and swooning air and carried the shadows of the dancers and the bulbous turbans of the servants floating and spinning and fading and reforming past the great golden oblongs of the ballroom windows.

As the little boat drew further off into the night, an exact reflection of the magical and triangular city hung in the still water like a bright honeycomb. Joining along the line of the waterfront, the two towns grew together in a golden lozenge. The structure of the submarine city swayed for a few moments in the ripples left by the oars and then, as the soft dislocation subsided, cohered once more in silent and shining congruency.

But, away from the strangely resplendent town, the night ahead was black and forbidding. The sea beyond the coral bar was as motionless as the water inside the broken zone of lagoons that girdled the island, and the light of the ship, in spite of the long silent labour of the two oarsmen, remained as far away as ever. Plessis and its reflection shrank into a distant rhomboid. Looking back over her shoulder, Berthe saw that the flames of the Salpetrière, so angry and menacing a short time ago, had sunk once more below the crater's edge. The crater itself was only to be singled out by the faint pink undersides of the clouds of smoke that everlastingly streamed upwards into the dark. Outside the town, all on the island was black, except for the lantern of some belated, or early, traveller, climbing the steep track that led through the forest above Plessis and over the watershed to windwardside.

After an hour's silent rowing the light ahead began slowly to grow a little larger and Berthe, peering forward over the oarsmen's shoulders, thought she discerned a dark shape on the water between the skiff and its goal. Every so often it blotted out the ship's lantern. At first she thought that it might be an illusion, a result of her long scrutiny into the darkness ahead. But no, it appeared again, and the others, twisting their heads round, saw it as well. Resting on their oars a moment they could hear a faint and rhythmic splashing. Convinced that it was the boat carrying Josephine to the waiting vessel, they redoubled their efforts. After a while, Berthe lost track of it, but at last the ship began to appear with more distinctness. This belied their first fears that she was actually under way and creeping forward with whatever stray capful of wind might be loose over the motionless water. The port lantern hanging in the shrouds revealed that she was a schooner of considerable size. Her bowsprit, supported by a golden mermaid, pointed south. There was no sign of the smaller boat whose presence they had faintly perceived, and presumably the two runaways were by now on board. But the lack of wind had removed all hazard from the chase, and halting a minute, Sosthène and Berthe and Gentilien discussed what tactics they should follow.

If they were denied permission to board they would shout to Josephine and try to persuade her to return. If this should fail, or if Josephine were not allowed to talk to them, which could hardly be possible, they would row astern, learn the name of the schooner and severely harangue the captain and the crew; inform them of the guilty transaction to which—no doubt in all innocence!— they were making themselves accomplices; roundly summon them to surrender Josephine, after which, if they chose, they could sail away to the devil with the precious Sciocca. Failing this (they would shout) the pursuers could return to Plessis and follow them the moment the wind rose in the Count's cutter, and chase them wherever they went. If the calm lasted until they got to the shore they would return at once with a posse of police and if necessary, with the entire population of Plessis; seize Josephine from their midst, put every man jack aboard under arrest and impound the schooner—that is, if they could hold the population back from setting her on fire outright. In all these deliberations it was Sosthène who took the initiative and when they stooped over their oars again, Berthe could see, by the distant glow of Plessis, that his face had kindled with anticipation. When, almost alongside, he leant forward and touched her on the knee with the words 'on y va!', she saw that his teeth were bared in a smile.

But, instead of hostility, they were hailed by friendly greetings from a row of dark figures leaning over the side. The rope ladder was down, and, as it had been pre-concerted, Sosthène, followed by Gentilien and then by Berthe, sped up the wooden steps. A newly-lighted lantern, hung from the mast to supplement the port and starboard lights, revealed a schooner as white with salt-petre snow as though she were made of icing sugar and rigged with a web of rock-crystal. Gripping the shrouds – the sudden pressure shaking out clouds of snow from the ropes – they hoisted themselves over the bulwarks and jumped down to the schooner's deck.

'These three figures,' Berthe said, 'a French officer of oddly juvenile appearance with his uniform in rags, an elderly negro with powdered hair dressed in black velvet and gold lace and silver buckles like a Haitian king, and, lastly, a fair-haired young woman in an elaborate green taffeta ball dress and bare feet, suddenly materialising out of the night and alighting one after the other on the planks – the first two grasping cutlasses like a boarding party at the battle of Lepanto – struck wonder and bewilderment that were obviously unfeigned into the hearts of the little community that had formed a semi-circle in the lantern light.

'They were all negroes, and at their centre, with steel-rimmed spectacles shining on his long bony face, stood one of the tallest men I have ever seen. Behind him was standing a smaller man with a stone jar under his arm and three glasses clenched between the fingers of his out-stretched hand in a gesture of welcome. There was a long silence. The tall figure in spectacles was the first to recover. He raised a broad-brimmed hat and shook hands with us in turn, bidding us gravely welcome in English to the schooner *Edith Fan* of Carriacou in the Grenadines[1], of which he, Roderick Graham, was Captain.

'It took less than two minutes' talk and a freely granted permission to look all over the ship to prove that nobody on board had the faintest idea of the matter in hand. The *Edith Fan* was on her way back from Basse-terre in Saint Kitts, where she had taken a cargo of the ponies that Captain Graham's brother, a Seventh Day Adventist like himself, bred in Carriacou. They had taken on a cargo of grain in Antigua on the return trip and had run into a dead calm as they passed Saint-Jacques a few hours earlier; and, when we came on board, they were waiting for the wind that often blows up an hour or two before daybreak. And what about the boat we had seen a quarter of an hour before? It turned

---

1. Carriacou is the largest of the Grenadine Islands, an archipelago of small islands lying between Grenada and St. Vincent in the British Wind-ward Islands, far to the south of Saint-Jacques. The inhabitants are of mixed Scottish and negro descent and they formerly talked with a noticeably Scottish accent.

out to have been a dug-out canoe full of Caribs, heading for Rosalie in Dominica; probably smugglers. They had passed under the schooner's bowsprit and there had been no white people on board. All the Captain said was quite plainly the truth. We believed him at once and our hearts sank.

'What, then, had happened to Josephine? She could not possibly hide in the island, so Sciocca must have planned some other way out. I remembered all of a sudden the light I had seen moving through the forest heading for the windwardside. Of course! I caught hold of Sosthène and Gentilien and leading them to the bulwarks, pointed to the black mountainside where the same light, considerably higher now, but still with a long climb to the watershed ahead of it, faintly glimmered – a far remoter will o' the wisp, it immediately struck me, even than the schooner's lantern had first seemed through the fan-topped window in Plessis.

'The high spirits that I thought I had divined in Sosthène just before we boarded the schooner, which had, rather naturally, subsided for a moment at the total failure of our expedition, suddenly, and, to me inexplicably at first, revived at this sudden sharp twist in our affairs. The plan of elopement became as plain as daylight as Sosthène explained it, and Gentilien and I nodded in agreement as his eager voice reconstructed the flight. The Governor had a summer holiday-house on windwardside at Anse Caraïbe, which is exactly where the watershed path led. It was here that the Government House yacht, the *Felix Faure*, lay per-

manently at anchor in the only natural harbour on the
Atlantic coast of Saint-Jacques. He must have arranged
for horses to be waiting at some distance outside the
town at three o'clock, where he had appointed a rendez-
vous. Just over the watershed at the Etang du Cacique –
a hamlet on the edge of a bottomless tarn below the
Chaudières – a change of horses would be waiting, or a
pony-trap a league and a half further on, where the
mountain path rejoined the coast road that looped all the
way – too long to cover during the hours of night-time
– round the south of the island. And from there it was
only one and a half hours to where they could weigh
anchor and be off. And then where? Dominica was too
near – Cousin Agénor was a friend of the English
Governor, and they would be equally easy to trace in
Guadeloupe, the Saints, or Marie Galante, or Martinique. No, they would either head further north through
the Faives islets to Antigua, Monserrat, Nevis or St Kitts,
and thence through the Greater Antilles to Mexico or
the United States; or south to St Lucia, St Vincent,
Grenada, or Trinidad, to disappear into Venezuela and
the South American Republics. In fact, once out of the
Leeward or the Windward Islands, they were lost.

'"We must stop them before they leave Jacobean
waters," Sosthène urged.

'"And we can. With any luck I'll reach Anse Caraïbe
by the Piton d'Esnambuc path before the wind rises and,
if not, I will chase them in one of the fishing-boats there.
Gentilien, you must come ashore with me and take a
horse north to Cap d'Ivry and get one of the sloops to

put to sea to watch the Northern route. Even if Messieurs Gontran and François are as drunk as Mademoiselle Berthe says, we'll get one of them to write you a letter to the bailiff – though I don't think you would need one; they all know you." He turned to me and said, "And the Southern route, Berthe, is yours." Before I could speak he had led us both over to the coil of rope where Captain Graham was sitting. Avoiding unnecessary details, he told him what was afoot and said that, though none of us had a centime with us, if he would trust us, his help would be well rewarded. The help we needed was this: would he, when the wind rose, sail the *Edith Fan* down to Cap d'Estaing, the southernmost point on the island, with me, and intercept the *Felix Faure* or any craft heading down the east coast for the Windwards?

'There was something very urgent and convincing in Sosthène's manner, but nevertheless I was astonished when the Captain nodded his long spectacled head and consented. Three of the crew were Jacobeans and the sailor who had offered us the rum as we boarded turned out to be one of the Count's numerous godsons, fittingly named Agénor. He had not seen Sosthène for years and, though he had wondered all along if it were he, had hesitated to ask. After joyful recognitions, Sosthène and Gentilien prepared to set off. Captain Graham was even persuaded to let them have Agénor and the two other Jacobeans to help row the skiff back more quickly to the Mouillage. Sosthène's sudden impetuous energy, his communicative and friendly authority, the speed and resolution of everything he did, were such that the whole schooner was infected. As I watched him pointing out on the chart the waters round Cap d'Estaing, indicating the likeliest inlets for us to lie in wait and the reefs where the enemy could most effectively be cornered, I wondered if this could be the same Sosthène who, ever since his return from France, had talked to me so desperately of self-destruction. Was this the sad young man that lay all day under the mango trees of Beauséjour with a volume of Vauvenargues or Seneca? The prospect of action had swept away the cloud of doubt, or melancholy and abstraction in which Sosthène had seemed to be wandering and turned him in a second into something swift, determined and mercurial.

'The three sailors and Gentilien were soon down the ladder. I embraced Sosthène, who followed them at once into the boat. The face that looked back over the tiller was transfigured with ardour. Swift strokes carried the skiff out of the lantern's range. Cheerful shouts and the valedictory gleam of a flourished cutlass answered our cries of *good luck* as the darkness hid them.

'The second journey, with twice the number of oarsmen on board, was much faster than the first; but it seemed to last an eternity as I leaned over the bulwarks. Although the schooner was some way out to sea, the beat of drums and the sound of violins from the ballroom floated clearly across the water. Through the Captain's spy-glass I followed the itinerary of the lantern on the mountainside. The footpath climbed in a long zigzag to a point where the forest ended in a stony ridge of pumice and basalt scree between the crater of the Salpetrière and Morne d'Esnambuc. There was still a long climb ahead. The road Sosthène prepared to take to Anse Caraïbe lay across the steep, brittle side of Morne d'Esnambuc and along a tortuous ledge hacked out of the tufa which overhung a deep and dangerous canyon : a journey full of hazards on foot, still more perilous in the dark on the back of Haïdouk, the fast Cuban horse he planned to take from the stables. Just as the lantern turned the last angle of its climb the small dark silhouette of the boat appeared in the gold triangle under Plessis and broke the reflected town. I saw them land at the Mouillage and plunge uphill into the frenzied rigadoon with which the whole town was blocked, and begin to fight their way through the revolving wings and antlers in the Place Hercule. In a few moments they had vanished.'

A flag in the music from the Serindan house drew the aim of Berthe's telescope to the crest of the town. The ballroom was emptying through the open windows into the garden and the circumference of the spy-glass's end revealed the terraces crowded with small figures. Then a new kind of music began. Berthe's spirits, infected by Sosthène's enthusiasm and by the feeling that Josephine was not lost, had risen buoyantly. Now, at the sound of one of the Count's 'surprises' she was filled with an odd and overflowing access of happiness. At these new sounds the jangling percussion, the distant and muted booming of carnival, fell silent, and the countless whirling torches of Plessis came to rest. The clear sad sound of French hunting horns sailed into the stillness of the night. Somewhere in that far off lighted circle, the three *piqueux* of the Count's pack from Beauséjour were standing under the leaves in their scarlet coats, their black cheeks expanded over the mouthpieces of their slender and curling instruments, sending over the waters of the Antilles notes that set ghostly finger-tips creeping up the nape of Berthe's neck under the thick and disordered pile of plaits. The fanfare played the children's song about the Good King Dagobert, then the sequence of the grave and formal little tunes, so unlike the brisk twanging of English hunting horns, which mark the incidents of the chase in France as solemnly as the movements in a pavane. They rang in the distance like the secret voice of all French forests; the spirit of the tapestried and the unicorn-haunted penumbra of their alleyways and of the great druidical trees when the bare winter branches are clouded with mistletoe.

The strains and anxieties of the night and the fever of the pursuit were quieted for a moment and Berthe, thus compellingly and without warning reminded, as the notes of the Appel and the Hallali reached her ears, of a girlhood that seemed a century ago, of long rides beside her father in the Vendean woods and of the squat rustic towers of her home, felt her eyes misting and the twinkling town of Plessis growing indistinct at the other end of the spy-glass. The sad notes of the Saint Hubert and then of the Death died away at last and left that nocturnal world, for the first time for several nights and days, in silence.

Captain Graham and the sailors were now leaning over the bulwarks on either side of Berthe and peering at the capital over which this strange hush had fallen. Before any of them uttered a word or a single sound of carnival had broken out on the shore, a thin swaying pencil-stroke of silver began slowly ascending from the apex of the town and up into the darkness where it expanded in a great shining dome of light composed of bright falling and radiating threads that hung in the middle of the air like a floating palace. A long gasp of wonder escaped the seamen as they watched the firework subsiding, and, seconds later, at the same moment that the cracks of the explosion reached the schooner across the expanse of water, came the massed thousands of exclamations from Plessis in a single cadence that died away like the sighing of a giant. Each sinking thread of fire opened in a cupola that drooped seawards in a silver harebell to meet the reflected upturned cups of light that rose through the intervening fathoms to compose with them loose and shrinking armillary spheres of radiance that the salt water soon extinguished. Then a golden sheaf of grouped rockets soared upwards and spread, blown higher, it might almost seem, by the delayed and muffled gasp that its ascension detonated; to break up, as each trajectory began to curve towards its fall, into a shower of coloured balls that slowly drifted downwards to meet their climbing under-water ghosts, and kiss there for a moment on the surface and expire.

The bangs echoed volleying through the twisted island ravines like the sounds of a battle far away. Rocket followed rocket, flinging their coloured fragments over the water in broken rainbows, and soon, at their roots, the battlements of the round tower were a burning ring of Catherine Wheels and the tiered and statued terraces were spouting with scores of Roman Candles. The shadowless lilac moonlight of magnesium irradiated the snow-town and the still and gorgon-struck citizens, and the gibbous and feathery upheaval of the mornes reared stage-wings that faded fast into the dark. When they had burnt themselves out a great silver rain was showered in the air, and then, against its slowly falling background, three perfect, immense and golden fleurs de lys burned for long seconds in a shimmering and visionary flag that slowly faded and then died, the reports and the loud valedictory cries lasting for many seconds after it had gone.

Berthe smiled in the darkness at the thought of the delight with which her cousin must have hoisted these airy lilies and she could imagine his tall figure, his brain filled with whirling oriflammes and Heaven knew what ancient war cries, with arms akimbo in the upward gazing throng as he jubilantly watched the proscribed emblems so brightly and triumphantly burning; and when she imagined the displeasure of the Governor, the ecstatic exclamations of the creoles, the unpartisan wonder of the negroes and the amusement of the Captain, she found herself laughing out loud. But the music had begun again and the wire-thin harmonies of the violins were sounding as the minute figures beyond the circular lens pressed back into the ballroom and began rhythmically to revolve past the windows in yet another waltz. All the clatter of carnival revived, the quasi-heraldic head-dresses gyrated once more and the fluttering groves of flambeaux were on the move again.

Though they had faded away two minutes before, the bright phantoms of these lilies seemed still to be hanging before her eyes when the dim disc at the far end of the spy-glass was suddenly turned, as though by the igniting of a last and cataclysmic firework, into a blinding and incandescent ball of light. She felt the alarmed grip of Captain Graham's hand on her shoulder and then two seconds later came a deafening clap of thunder as though the world had been blown in two. The night had vanished. Everything was suddenly brighter than noonday and from the crater of the Salpetrière a broad pillar of red and white flame, thickly streaked with black, was shooting into the sky like the fire from a cannon's mouth. It climbed higher every second until it had reached a fierce zenith miles up in the air, and the roar that accompanied its journey was interrupted by hoarse thunder claps that almost broke the eardrum. A great wave of heat, as though an oven door had been opened, swept over the watchers on the schooner, and the sea, reflecting the conflagration, leapt from the darkness in a smooth and vivid desert. The neighbouring islands of Marie Galante, the Saints, Guadeloupe and Dominica, thus strangely lit up and towering all at once across the intervening leagues, looked almost within touching distance. Fiery fragments from the centre of the earth were flying through the sky and missiles like jagged lumps of fire, coming apart in their flight as liquidly as sealing wax, fell dripping to the water, whose smooth surface was broken up in a moment with a forest of waterspouts and plumes of steam. One of them, about the size, Berthe said, of a hayrick, fell about fifty yards to starboard and set the schooner rocking in a hot cloud of vapour. In a few seconds the blast that held this great flame as rigid as a plumbline from the sky to the over-flowing crater must have slackened, for the fiery column began to waver and its summit sank swelling and spread-ing from its height in great subsiding coils.

The forests and the canefields were burning savagely in a score of places and five great fires had broken out in Plessis itself. In the streets, all was panic and turmoil. Antlered and horned figures were leaping into the water and swarming aboard the sloops, and the terraces round the Serindan house were black with dancers in flight. A tall figure silhouetted above the burning town – could it be the Count's? it was impossible to distinguish through the spy-glass – had leapt on to the topmost balustrade and seemed, by the wild and quixotic flourishes of his arms, to be exhorting the fleeing throng not to give way to panic. Gaze as she might, it was no longer possible to pick out the faint lantern's gleam from the hundred fires in the forest, and, paralysed with horror, Berthe thought of the horses rearing and whin-neying, of Josephine, still dressed as a black hidalgo, flung this way and that in the heaving saddle among the crackling and blazing trunks, while the flames, tempestuously travelling, roared through the labyrinthine debris of those combustible woods. . . .

The great column had sunk almost level with the crater and the daylight radiance dwindled to a ghastly crimson glow as the flames curled from the volcano's lip in a shrinking cauliflower of fire. Some of the crater's wall must have fallen in and blocked the channel. It looked as if the eruption were over.

All these events had happened in the space of seconds and Berthe was still gazing petrified at the dark patch in the burning forest, where she prayed that Josephine might still be alive, when a second blinding flash burst from exactly that place, followed by something which seemed for a moment, by contrast, pitch darkness. For a black cloud had burst out of the volcano's flank far below the crater. The fires inside the mountain had blown a new rift which spread upwards towards the streaming *chaudières*. This jagged, growing tear revealed the inside of the mountain for a blazing fraction of a second before it was obscured by the rapidly swelling volume of a cloud that came rolling and billowing down towards the town, setting fire to everything in its track. There was a heavy and pillow-soft inevitability in the movements of these oily black convolutions and, now and then, as they rolled forward, they seemed to hang like the folds of a curtain, with a satanic light flickering in the changing pleats. Then it moved onwards again, heavy and swelling, and sometimes breaking open for a second or two to show the white and orange whorls of fire that raged inside.

A deep rumbling groan accompanied this journey of destruction. Now and again the dark mass would kindle from inside, and the black sails of smoke glowed crimson and scarlet and then changed to a soft pink without the seething interior flames once breaking through the containing folds, which momentarily appeared as thin and transparent as the surface of a balloon. At last the entire cloud was growing from the island's side in a great unfolding rose. It slowly faded again into fire-rimmed blackness and all was opaque and impenetrable. Gently it settled over the town and enfolded the houses and the spires.

The streets had fallen silent. The citizens had been halted in their flight and then laid low in swathes, as though one invisible sweep of a sickle had reaped them all, by the descending gas which had invaded the capital the moment the mountain-side opened. The flaming Serindan house was the first to disappear and then the black tide flowed wreathing and eddying over the roofs and down the alleyways. Long before it reached the waterfront, Berthe could see the slender dolphin lamp posts drooping like dying flowers before they finally melted away. The ships caught fire and the burning masts and hulls glowed redly for a moment through the cloud as it rolled out over the bay. The flames deepened to scarlet and purple, then they too were hidden in darkness.

Soon the whole island was obscured in the black and all-enveloping volume which, now fed ceaselessly from behind by the widening rent in the side of Saint-Jacques, rose high in the air in a dark flickering wall. Hot black ash as fine as soot had begun to rain over the schooner and an overpowering smell of sulphur filled the variable twilight. The Captain and the sailors and Berthe had fallen to their knees long ago and, against the crackling and groaning of the hidden conflagration, she could hear their deep voiced wavering prayers. As the cloud spread over the water and the furnace-like heat advanced, the speed of the prayers grew and the pitch of the Captain's voice rose. Sometimes, for a few seconds, the world was in darkness except for the burning sparks that flew from Plessis and the forests. The whole sky was now afloat with them. The bank of cloud would flicker from inside with an upheaval of the burning gases it contained. Then lightning began to shower to and fro. Sometimes it was held captive within the cloudbank, illuminating its incandescent concavity with a shuddering electric glare, and sometimes it burst forth helterskelter into the night in branching prongs and zigzags that fissured the sky's surface and lighted for a wild second or two the great quaking pile and the empty sea and the faces of the sailors shining under rivers of sweat. Close over their heads they could hear the disordered wingbeats and the alarmed cries of birds. Some of them collided with the masts and the rigging and perched in the stays, or, overcome by the gaseous fumes loosed all round Saint-Jacques, fell lifeless to the deck and over the surrounding water. A brief outburst of light from the shifting cloud-stack revealed a ragged troop of flamingoes among the floating motes, flown there from the high pools of the forest. Soon they too were hidden in the universal gloom.

Berthe sank into silence at this point of her story. 'It is hard to convey,' she finally went on, 'the speed of all this. It takes a long while to tell and it seemed to last an eternity at the time, but I don't think that more than half an hour can have passed between the first perpendicular uprush of fire and this mobile semi-darkness. We watched the black shape in a state of helpless astonishment. The whole of Saint-Jacques was in dissolution and our only course was to wait until the growing circumference of this terrible cloud should swallow up the *Edith Fan* and its shipload of mercifully asphyxiated corpses. For the sulphurous reek was growing stronger every minute and the volcanic dust kept raining down. Until we bandaged our mouths and noses in cloths dipped in brine, it seemed likely to choke us. All wild and momentary thoughts of survival and rescue for anyone on the island which may have leapt into our heads when the first outbreak stopped were abolished by the appalling completeness of what happened afterwards. It seemed inevitable that the cloud should overtake us and, when a new and strange commotion – a sound of rushing and whirling – began in the air above us and an increasing clamour among the birds, we thought the moment had come. The Captain's prayers ("O Lord, look down on thy children of Israel, shed Thy mercy on them and save them from the flames") rose in a long cry of despair. But the air began to lose its fearful heat and the fall of burning soot grew thinner. The cloud's soft progress over the water halted and its edges began to creep backwards again as though the ghostly mass were drawing in its skirts. It lifted from the sea and, flowing back on itself in an immense and uniformly evolving coil encompassing the island, the entire shadowy mass, spiked with lightning and accompanied by claps of thunder, rolled into the sky and joined the rain-clouds which had hung motionless there for days.

'All was suddenly light again. The sea was a brilliant disc and the surrounding archipelago reappeared. From the shore to the crest of the Salpetrière, the island was ablaze. The sudden uprush of wind gathered and combed the flames into a roaring scarlet shock of hair streaked with black tresses of soot from half a dozen new holes torn in the sides of the mountain and climbed blazing and winding upwards. A cool breath of wind from the open sea crossed the schooner's deck in the direction of the island and then, growing in strength every second, broke up the sea into great waves. One of them lifted the vessel skywards and sent her with a lurch into a hollow and then to the top of another tall hill of water. We had all risen from our knees to grasp the shrouds or the bulwarks for support. At that moment the groaning of the fires from the island grew to a fierce crackling roar and the huge tangle of flames fanned over to one side and stretched away southwest.

'Plessis, clear all at once of the smoke and the obscuring wall of flames, was unrecognisable. Only the scarlet bones of the Serindan house remained, a few broken walls of Government House, two gutted belfries, the round bastions and the lighthouse and one or two of the statues. The rest had vanished. The streets were choked with a burning igneous rubble or they had become rivers of lava which flowed steaming and hissing into the sea. Every valley had turned into one of these sluggish streams of fire and the shape of the island itself appeared to have changed. Even the rocks, those great bare shoulders of tufa and basalt jutting through the flattened blaze of the forests, shone red hot. Watching the steady horizontal drift of the flames, the sailors realised what had happened long before I did. "Praise the Lord!" the Captain shouted. "The Lord's name be in my mouth for evermore!" The sailors were flying up the rigging and their voices sounded from mast to mast as they moved along the spars. The sails were flung free and each expanse of canvas filled with a smack until the red night overhead was crowded with canvas that flapped for a moment and then bellied taut. The Captain was twirling the wheel and bringing the bowsprit round till it pointed due west. The swinging booms were made fast and the *Edith Fan* bounded across the waves. For the Trade Winds had revived.

'We had not travelled far before voices hailed us out of the night. A sailor, peering over the red waves from the bows, cried that there were some men in the water. Cables and ladders were lowered over the side and soon ten half-naked men were dripping on the deck. They were the Caribs. A lump of falling scoria had hit their dugout canoe, miraculously without harming anyone. They had all leapt overboard. But the sides had been burnt half away so they had capsized her and clung to the wreck in hopes of being rescued. I had never seen any Caribs before – only a few hundred of them still survived, in Dominica. They were bronze-coloured men with beautiful, rather mongoloid faces and long black hair cut in a thick fringe above heavy-lidded eyes. They scarcely uttered a word, beyond saying that they had felt "Salpetrière was going up", but huddled to-gether at the foot of the mizzen-mast. They were the descendants of the cannibal savages that inhabited this archipelago long before the whites or the blacks arrived. Some unconscious and atavistic wisdom had prompted them to escape, just as it had prompted the iguanas and the snakes and the armadilloes, while the black and the white intruders had received, or at least, had taken, no hint of the disasters ahead. These primitive men had an inborn knack of survival when dealing with their ancestral problems which was lacking in everybody else . . .

'The flames, meanwhile, were all driving south-west-wards and as the schooner drew away, we could see the great barrier of smoke stretching from the leaning bon-fire across bright miles of sea in the direction of the windward slopes of Dominica. As I gazed back over the poop through the spy-glass, the island itself appeared all at once to be moving. The southern side was slipping lower in a smooth white-hot subsidence, until, accom-panied by a long rumble of fire and falling rock, the entire mass of Morne d'Esnambuc – the forested peak where we had so often picnicked – began to fall away. Used as my eyes had become that night to strangeness and horror, I thought that they or my mind must have been affected. But the cries of the sailors proved that it was no illusion. The island was coming apart. The fissure that had spread from the watershed between the Morne and the Salpetrière was opening in a fiery yawn. As the jaws widened a long orange tongue of flame curled out and lazily upwards and then twisted away into the current of the trade winds. Morne d'Esnambuc, split now from the watershed to the sea, tilted outwards. Its base was giving. Slowly the overhanging peak broke away and overturned with a shattering detonation and an avalanche of many million tons of red hot mineral. Immense burning bits detached themselves and rolled thundering through the forests or bounded far from the island while the main body of the mountain turned through a slow arc of ninety degrees and collapsed into the sea in the heart of an enormous rising palisade of water and steam.

'A tidal wave threw the schooner this way and that with a violence that threatened to break her timbers apart, then fled away towards the horizon in a widening ring. The steady drive of the Trade Winds carried us further off and everything began changing fast. Flames were pouring from the exposed heart of the mountain, a wall of vapour now surrounded the broken island and the hiss of steam was almost as loud as the roar and the crackle of the flames. As the distance increased and the blur of steam grew thicker it got harder to see the details of what was happening. Saint-Jacques was now reduced to a steep red triangle growing rapidly smaller; more rapidly, in fact, than seemed natural until I realised that Saint-Jacques was sinking into the ocean.

'Every few minutes the sea was ploughed up into ravines of water that looked ready to engulf the ship. Then the sea would lift her, shaking and flooded, to the summit of another great wave. Once she was drawn into a hollow that turned her three times round on herself in a whirlpool before a heavier onrush of water from the east came and lifted her free. Less of the island was visible through the spy-glass at the end of each of these contests. Soon only the cone of the Salpetrière remained above the water, which had now grown unnaturally still. A long fierce flame curling from the crater proved that one channel had remained free of the encroaching salt water, which had sealed the others one by one with hissing explosions of steam. At last only the crater's rim remained above sea level. Then, as we all gazed at the distant red circle and its immense plume of fire, the crater tilted over slowly on its side and the water flowed in and snuffed it almost in silence; and, of course, for ever. The night had been growing darker fast until the wild glare had dwindled to a blood red glow. The unnatural daylight of an hour before had shrunk to a solitary branching flower of yellow flame, which, severed from its stalk now, floated loose in the sky along the tide of the wind, which drew it lengthways into the shape of a flying dragon. The dragon grew smaller and redder and turned into a flower again and slowly fell to pieces until only a few crimson flickers remained; and when the last floating chrysanthemum petal went out, we were in the dark. The waves from this last motion of the distant submarine earthquake shook the sea all round us into a storm again and the schooner plunged in the darkness. High overhead and as remote as the Milky Way, the sky was covered by a faint red confetti of small drifting cinders. This was all that remained of the island of Saint-Jacques des Alisées, its mountains and its forests, its beautiful town and the forty-two thousand souls that had lived there till an hour ago. The world had come to an end. *Solvet saeclum in favilla!*'

*   *   *

The silence that followed Berthe's last words was unusually long.

'My mind took a long time,' she resumed at last, 'to catch up with all that I had seen. There must be a merciful kind of stupidity, almost an anaesthetic, that settles on one's brain at moments like this and limits the range of one's understanding to the bare faculties of sight and sound and touch. I saw the flames and the smoke, heard the explosions and felt the heat; knew, in a theoretical way, that all the people I loved and every inhabitant of the island had been killed, that the island had blown up and sunk to the bottom of the sea; but all as a sleep-walker or somebody in the power of a drug might understand these things. Various detached and almost static visions kept reappearing before my mind's eye like lantern-slides: the first upright flames, and then, like one of the sieges or disasters in a picture by Gustave Doré, the thousands of figures locked in flight down the streets of Plessis and the Serindan terraces. Next the great rose-like cloud turning black, the hecatomb of the islanders, the lamp-posts melting, the smoke coiling upwards, the fall of Morne d'Esnambuc and lastly the flames dying away after the volcano had been swallowed up. The only fact that I was able to assimilate for a time was the immense, the blind and brutal and annihilating event of the island's destruction: a thing so irresistible and in-different to ordinary life that the death of the Jacobeans and my own survival seemed a matter of trivial, almost frivolous lack of consequence. Eruptions and cataclysms and plagues and the colliding of planets were the only real, the only inevitable events, and the human activities that happened to lie in their path, and which are destroyed with such blind ease and ignorance, were of as little real importance as the doings of insects. How effortlessly they had all been burnt up! How pointless all our passions and complications and the intricate struc-ture of our little society now seemed! We were reduced by this juxtaposition of unbridled power and absolute impotence to the status of ants and, by these standards, the destruction of forty-two thousand of them seemed as slight and, fundamentally, as uninteresting, a matter, as the fluke by which one of them had escaped: a stray ant had survived when the whole nest was demolished by a power that was unaware of the existence of either ants or nest. That was all. Explosions, floods and ice ages, you might say, are the only true dates in history and the improvisations of human societies between these events – art, civilisation, love, wars, literature, the development and the melting of one religion into another, the movement of ideas, the migrations of power from continent to continent – have as little bearing on this basic calendar of red letter days as a page out of Fabre's Book of Insects. Then how microscopic, how minute, were the feuds, the passions, the pleasures and the vanities of the small anachronistic community of Saint-Jacques!'

Berthe's lighter twinkled on the other side of the table as she surrounded herself with smoke once more and I heard the momentary rather pleasant grate of her laugh. 'I don't pretend that I shaped my thoughts at the time even as coherently as this. But they were the half-conscious ideas, I think, composing the anodyne of fatalism and despair that carried me through the first pains of this amputation.

'But slowly, as the effects of the shock wore off, this changed. The eruption shrank to the size of an insane and wicked interruption, an unnatural accident which had inflicted a cruel and undeserved death on all the people I loved, and broken and drowned the world we had lived in. The disaster seemed as wanton as the blows and tramplings of some immense and muscular idiot. For a long time, a very long time afterwards, Saint-Jacques and its inhabitants were the only real things for me, and the outside world a shadowy limbo. I felt as a solitary surviving inhabitant of Atlantis might have felt when his foothold had vanished under the waves.

'I tried to work out a theory that the disaster might have been a solution from Heaven to a tangle that could only have unravelled itself otherwise in a sequence of lesser tragedies: a sort of mass solution, in fact. But I soon abandoned this. Any thought of a celestial visitation, like the fate that befell the wicked cities in the Old Testament, was equally unprofitable, for if anything, the inhabitants of Saint-Jacques, in spite of the slightly queer form of society that had sprung up there, were kinder and better, as they were certainly happier, than in most other parts of the world. I remember wondering, too, if there were any supernatural purpose in the island gathering its own together – Sosthène, for instance, and Gentilien and the three Jacobean sailors – for this culminating holocaust; while the Caribs and I were allowed to escape. The inclusion of the Captain and Government House in the disaster ruled this out at once. In fact, there was no lesson, no consoling moral to be drawn. Except, perhaps, that although there may be a curious kind of mutual magnetism between people and the things that happen to them in ordinary circumstances, these great tragedies (whether brought on by human agency or what is sometimes called the Hand of God) spare and condemn with a lack of purpose that no law, divine, human or natural, can possibly rationalise. They are irrelevancies. As the eruption and all its details and implications slowly overcame my first stupid but merciful insensibility, all trace of fatalism melted away and left nothing but utter misery and anger and despair. I felt that my survival had been a desertion. I hated myself for being alive and wished that I had died with them in the flames.'

'What happened,' I asked her after a pause, 'in the end?'

'How do you mean, "in the end"?' she asked.

'After the island had disappeared?'

'Oh,' her voice sounded very tired. 'It's not very interesting. We sailed on in the dark. There was a great wind and at last, though it cannot have been above an hour after the last flame had disappeared, dawn began to break. It was a crimson and violet blur in the east, brightening through the falling soot and cinders into all the colours of the spectrum, though the light was as dim as that in mid winter in northern Europe. The sea was discoloured with soot and mud and afloat with branches and debris and sargasso weed and with hundreds of dead fish and dead or tired birds.

'Day broke only just in time, for our many gyrations had driven the *Edith Fan* off her course and carried her within a mile of the northern rocks of Dominica, under a cape called Pointe Baptiste. Another half an hour of darkness would have wrecked her there. The Caribs and I asked to be put ashore, so Captain Graham sailed in close and landed us in a dinghy which they lowered from the deck. A crowd of creole-speaking negroes helped us ashore, the Caribs set off at a trot towards their forests, and the schooner sailed away. The negroes surrounded me and I had to answer a hundred questions, for the events of the night had filled all the neighbouring islands with terror and dismay. The horizon where

Saint-Jacques had been the nearest landmark was now an empty sweep of sea disfigured by an enormous clay-coloured smear.'

For the inhabitants of these wild northern reaches of Dominica, it occurred to me, the descent of this fair-haired girl, barefoot in a tattered ball dress, soaking and smeared with soot, and without a possession in the world, alone among strangers on this strange morning, must have seemed an event almost as untoward. An old negress called Victoria took pity on her, put her arm round her shoulders and carried her to her hut out of range of the questioners. Putting her on a bed of palm branches, she gave her a long drink of coconut milk. Then, laying one hand on Berthe's forehead, and taking one of Berthe's hands with the other, she told her gently to go to sleep.

'Victoria looked after me,' Berthe said, 'for a whole month and nursed me through a terrible fever. I used to lie all day long in a hammock strung up between the pimento trees on the headland by her hut at Pointe Baptiste. It overlooked a sandy bay and coral reefs littered with conch shells and the waste of water, which gradually cleared as the days went by, where the mountains of Saint-Jacques had once floated. In the end, Victoria gave me some clothes and took me to the little harbour of Portsmouth and then accompanied me on the boat to the island capital of Roseau. The French Consulate and the British Administrator and the nuns were very kind to me. There was no news of a single survivor from Saint-Jacques. Every soul had perished except me. Ships sailing over the point had found no traces of the island and repeated soundings proved that it must have sunk to a very great depth.

'With the help of these new friends I made my way to Martinique and French Guiana and finally to Brazil, where I joined a Sisterhood of Poor Clares as an oblate. I stayed with them, working in the slums of Bahia and at various towns up the Amazon, for nearly ten years. I thought for a long time that I would never recover from the shock of Saint-Jacques and the feeling of loss and loneliness that followed its disappearance. But I did – sufficiently at least, for outward appearances. I loved this hard work with the nuns. But I grew restless. So I left them in the end and began giving lessons in Rio. But I longed to live on an island again, so I made my way to the South Seas and then back to Europe and the Mediterranean Islands – I seem to have worked through them all in my time. I got a job as a nurse in France during the first war. Finally I settled here. I hope I shall never live anywhere else. A few years before the last war I inherited a small sum of money – just enough to see me out, I think. So I only give lessons for pleasure now – I have always enjoyed teaching. And here I am still.'

Her voice sounded tired out. The moon was setting, and the Pleiades, crossing the middle of the sky, would soon follow her. It was a late hour of the night.

'How strange it is,' she said, as we stood up, stretching our limbs, 'that a whole island and all the lives on it can vanish without a trace.'

'Not quite without a trace,' I said.

'How do you mean?' Berthe asked.

'Last year when I was in Dominica and Guadeloupe, fishermen told me that anyone, crossing the eastern channel between the islands in carnival time, can hear the sound of violins coming up through the water. As though a ball were in full swing at the bottom of the sea.'

'Do they?' Berthe's voice had changed entirely. There was a note of surprise and of almost girlish excitement in her voice. In that fainting moonlight the ravaged and magnificent features appeared transfigured, and those grey eyes were suddenly faceted and sparkling under their heavy brows, which, usually frowning, had all at once unknit in two youthful arcs of astonishment and pleasure. 'Do they really say that?'

'Yes. They are called the "violins of Saint-Jacques" or just "the count's violins". Very little is known of the story now and it is seldom connected with the eruption; and, to judge from the way they speak, it might all have happened centuries ago. They say they are the fiddles that were played once at a great ball long ago given by a Count in honour of his beautiful daughter.'

Berthe seemed too moved to speak. At last she said, 'Thank you. Thank you so much for telling me that.' I felt certain that if I could have seen her eyes they would have been full of tears. In a few moments she held out her hand under the shadows of an olive tree to say good-night and turned away to the path that led to the camp bed where she slept out in summer under the vine-trellis. I took the pathway through the olives that led to the cliff's edge. Turning back, I could see her tall solitary figure standing by an ilex among the vines. She lifted her hand and waved and I climbed down the cliff through the arbutus and tamarisk to the glimmering seashore. The moon, in dying, had revived the faint radiance of the stars, but by the time I reached the town they too were fading, and a faint golden wing of light in the east was darkening and hardening the intervening mountain-tops of Asia Minor.

*   *   *

Early next morning, the captain of the caïque whose departure for Constantinople I had been awaiting for two weeks suddenly decided to set sail. There was no time to go and say good-bye to Berthe so I wrote a hasty letter of farewell at a café on the waterfront and sent a little bootblack pattering off with it over the cobbles. I went on board with my luggage, and settled in the bows.

Several hitches held up the caïque's departure, but the engines started at last, the mainsail was hoisted, the anchor was hauled on board. Turning her nose towards Turkey, the caïque sailed every moment faster through the anchored labyrinth of vessels. All at once we heard a shout from the quay. It was Phrosoula, running barefoot along the water's edge and frantically waving. The Captain cut off the engine, but the sail still kept the vessel in motion.

'This is from Kyria Mpertha!' Phrosoula shouted and threw a small parcel which I managed to catch.

Phrosoula's waving figure grew smaller as the caïque turned to the open sea again and the Anatolian Hills.

The parcel contained a spoon of elaborate design. Round it was wrapped a letter in Berthe's firm clear handwriting. *In haste* [it began]. *I wonder if you would like this, it is rather a curious present. Do you remember that I told you I found I was still holding a spoon when I fell over the armadillo? I must have tucked it into the front of my dress because when I went to bed in Victoria's hut (the kind old negress who took care of me in Dominica), there it was, with Josephine's crumpled letters, which you saw. They were all that remained of Saint-Jacques. I have kept it ever since and now I'd like you to have it.*

The long slender spoon was made of heavy silver. The stem was slightly bent, and where it expanded to form the handle, there was a scroll on which the word *Terpsichore* was incised. Still higher up, a small silver statuette in swaying draperies advanced at a dancing step and her tiptoes rested on either end of the scroll. A silver garland flew in a final curve between her upheld and elegantly twisted arms. It was an object at the same time both charming and engagingly comic. *The spoon* [Berthe's letter went on], *was one of a set of nine and the figurines were copied from sketches my cousin made of the statues placed along the wall of the terrace at Plessis. I hope I didn't tire you last night with my long rigmarole. It must be over fifty years since I inflicted it on anybody and I do not expect that I shall ever do so again. I am so grateful for what you told me about the violins and the ball for the Count's beautiful daughter. I have been thinking about it ever since and for some reason it has made me absurdly happy. It seems to make amends for much past unhappiness and it will never seem quite the same now; so I would like to send this small present in return.*

I am so glad, too, that there are no dates and names assigned to the violins and, above all, no link with the eruption. I hope Phrosoula catches you before your boat leaves and that you have a happy journey. Yours ever. Berthe.

Read more . . .

Patrick Leigh Fermor

A TIME OF GIFTS: ON FOOT TO CONSTANTINOPLE —
FROM THE HOOK OF HOLLAND TO THE MIDDLE DANUBE

The classic memoir of an enchanted journey across pre-war Europe

In 1933, at the age of eighteen, Patrick Leigh Fermor set off from the heart of London on an epic journey — to walk to Constantinople. It was to be a momentous experience, and one that would change the course of his life.

A Time of Gifts is the rich and sparkling account of his adventures as far as Hungary, after which *Between the Woods and the Water* continues the story to the Iron Gates that divide the Carpathian mountains and the Balkans. At once a coming-of-age memoir, an account of a journey, and a dazzling exposition of the English language, Patrick Leigh Fermor is acclaimed for his sweep, intelligence and observation, and the remarkable way in which he captures the moment in time.

'Nothing short of a masterpiece' Jan Morris

'A treasure chest of descriptive writing . . . The resplendent domes, the monasteries, the great rivers, the hospitable burgomasters, the sun on the Bavarian snow, the storks and frogs, the grandeurs, the courtesies, all are revealed with a sweep and verve that are almost majestic' *The Specator*

Order your copy now by calling Bookpoint on 01235 827716 or visit your local bookshop quoting ISBN 978-0-7195-6695-0
www.johnmurray.co.uk